THE WINGSWEPT SKY

DRAGONS OF AMONTYR
BOOK ONE

EVELYN GRIMALD STONE

TARNEY BRAE CREATIVE ENDEAVOURS

HUMAN
AUTHORED™
AG THE Authors Guild®

3371723

For everyone who wants nothing more than a quiet life
(preferably with dragons)

CONTENTS

AUTHOR'S NOTE

This book features a main character who is neurodivergent. I based her traits off of my own particular brand of sensory-avoidant autism. However, everyone's experience of autism and other neurodivergent characteristics are different, and this book should not be taken as a complete or exact depiction of everyone's experience.

This book also contains instances of discrimination based on neurodivergence and, in the case of dragons, breed. The characters do resolve these issues on page. The instances of ableism are based on personal experience.

Amontyr

SYNVAL

Ilisa

Virias

Dun Kennis

Balm Town

River Brim

CHAPTER 1

On the one day I needed to not be late, I was. Normally, my routine and internal clock were so in tune that I never needed to worry about waking up on time; I would rise with the dawn no matter the weather, no matter if I could see the sun. Last night, though, I had been too energised to sleep properly and now I was late.

Cursing, I shoved my legs into my new blue breeches, pulled my new blue tunic over my head, cinched a belt with my money pouch at my waist and yanked my boots on. I tugged my muddy brown hair into a long braid and hastily scrubbed my tan, freckled face in the washbasin before running from my room without a second glance.

I'd probably forgotten something.

A moment later, cursing again, I was back to snatch the heavy letter from its place on my dresser before darting out again. I skipped around my sister Carmen's youngest child, a boy of two, and waved a frantic hand at my mother, father, and grandmother, who were all gathered in the kitchen over the wood stove, waiting for the chicory to brew.

"Ay, Kayleigh, what are you—"

"Sorry, Mami, I'm late!"

I ignored the shouts that rang after me and ran for the door, leaping across the threshold and into the morning light. The sun was barely up over the horizon, leaving the landscape shrouded in mist, the trees and fields a green haze through it all. I ignored it all, ignored the beauty of the farm, the smell of the cows, the huff of the Grimble, the herding dragon, as I bounded past. I just ran.

I should have stayed the night in town, I grumbled to myself, already lengthening my stride and slowing my breath so that I could maintain the pace. Years of practise, of training, of obsessing over maps and routes and roads had led to this one thing. I was going to be a courier, and I was fast enough to be the best.

If I made it in time.

Ilisar rose up before me, the city a mass of stucco-and-stone buildings at the convergence of the two rivers. My family farm was located just outside the low walls that made up the boundaries of the city, so I'd been given special dispensation by the Courier Guild to stay there rather than in the city, provided I made it to work every day on time.

Today was my first day and already I was behind schedule.

I dodged wagons pulled by horses whose breath fogged. I leaped around merchants bringing in their wares for the covered market in the centre of the city. I shouted apologies to the two guard dragons who lounged on either side of the road into the city, their startled growls nearly making me stop and introduce myself properly. But, no, I had to be at the Guild Hall by the second bell of the day, which was set to go off any minute now.

I dug my feet into the hard-packed road and ran.

The Courier Guild Hall was situated at the eastern edge of the city, right beside a massive clearing bounded on one side by a large hill and the other by the river. It was a large complex, responsible for sorting the post, determining whether it went by foot courier, horse, or dragon, then assigning it to a courier and sending it out. There were stables with a veritable fleet of horses for swift delivery, and the hill had enough holes in it to house the dragons who had offered their service to the Guild.

I didn't care about the dragons or the horses. I wanted to *run*.

My whole life, I'd been running. Seeing the world as quickly as I could. Feeling the wind on my face. The joy of movement. I ran barefoot around my family's dairy farm since I could walk, racing from place to place, delivering messages from my father to my mother or my grandfather to my grandmother. My sister had been the proper one, the one happy to learn manners and graces and the things that made her welcome in any drawing room, all of which felt like grand mysteries to me. Instead, I'd poured over maps and memorised the details of the capital of Synval, noting alleys and thoroughfares, shops and residences. I could name any cross street in Ilisar, and all I'd ever wanted to do was trace the lines of those maps myself. To run those streets, delivering messages, packages, anything.

I had taken the Courier entrance exam two weeks ago and qualified, much to my father's delight and my mother's chagrin. Now, I was adorned in Courier blue and ready to get my assignment.

I slid onto the field outside the Hall just as the second bell of the day rang. There were about twenty other people there, and they all turned to look at me as I stopped, chest heaving. A group nearest the grassy field snickered, their leader a red-haired woman whose startled smirk only made her more striking.

"Glad you could join us," she said. I wasn't sure if she was being sarcastic, so I said nothing, only smiled. I was still catching my breath, I told myself. I wasn't being rude by ignoring the woman.

The group ranged outside the Hall were all wearing the blue tunic and breeches of the Couriers, all without the patches on the shoulder to denote what section they were in. New recruits, then. I was surprised at how many there were, and only about five were my age, twenty-two, the youngest the Guild allowed. The rest were older, some by ten years, some by more, some with brown skin, some with cream, the rest somewhere in between, though the mix of genders was fairly even.

I considered approaching a small group of people to see about checking in—or at least pretending to be sociable since people seemed to like me better when I pretended—when something flashed past my face, a blur of blue and heat and wings. I gasped and flinched backwards, bringing my hands up to protect my head. In turn, the small harrier dragon, no bigger than a kestrel, pulled back and hissed, claws raised.

"Windcatcher!" A man, about my age or a little older, ran in front of me, holding his hands up as he faced the dragon. He was dark-skinned, with brown hair that was nearly black, and rich, intense brown eyes. Handsome, if you were the sort to notice that type of thing. Which I wasn't. He flicked those eyes to me for a moment, assessing me, before he turned back to the dragon. I was surely about to combust with embarrassment, having such a reaction to a dragon. "You know you cannot simply fly off like that. Especially on today of all days."

The little dragon—Windcatcher—hovered in midair, her amber eyes whirling. Her blue hide was nearly the same colour as the courier tunic, and when she landed on her keeper's shoulder, she almost disappeared. Only the snaking of her neck and the twitch of her tail betrayed her.

"You have a dragon!" I blurted out. I winced. "Sorry. It's just—"

"Don't worry about it," the man said, smiling

that polite smile people—not me—seemed to throw about so easily. He shifted his shoulders so that the little harrier dragon could stretch her neck and sniff at me. "This is Windcatcher. She's nonverbal, but very friendly. She doesn't normally fly into people, but today is...a special occasion. I'm Andrés Mierza."

"Kayleigh Espinosa." I shifted my weight, not quite able to take my eyes from Windcatcher. "Nice to meet you."

Andrés's expression softened a touch. "Would you like to pet her?"

"Oh!" I blinked and pulled back, not quite sure when I'd leaned forwards to peer at the little dragon. I'd seen harrier dragons before, but I'd never been close enough to touch one. Most of my family's dragons were watch dragons, though there was also old Grimble, the herding dragon who managed the cows. They all tolerated me, but hated when I interrupted their work to ask questions about their scales or wings or what they liked to do when they weren't working. And they really hated my running about.

"Thank you," I murmured, lifting a hand. Windcatcher extended her head and preened as I scratched her chin. Her horns were sharp, but her hide was as soft as kid leather. "A pleasure to meet you, Windcatcher. You are a beautiful thing, aren't you?"

The little dragon bobbed her head and Andrés waited with a quiet smile. He watched me a little too intently. I felt my face heat under his scrutiny and tucked a strand of hair behind my ear. When were we going to check in and get our assignments? Or, really, how much small talk would I have to maintain with the intense dragon keeper before I was deliberately set aside?

"Are you hoping to be stationed as a dragon rider?" Andrés asked. There was something about the way he asked that had me shifting my attention from the harrier dragon to her keeper, my own too-observant eyes taking in every detail. The tense hold of his shoulders. The shining new boots. The flicker in his eyes that was too intent to be mere curiosity. The smile he wore, though, was perfectly natural to my eyes. I blinked and tried to flash a smile of my own.

"A rider?" I shook my head, realising he'd asked a question. "I want to be a foot messenger. I like to run."

Andrés nodded. "I can tell, the way you ran in here this morning."

I knew I was blushing furiously now. My attention slipped to the grass, the Guild hall, the other people lingering about. Anything to keep the prickling stare of Andrés off of me. I wondered again when the Guild official was to come and give out assignments. The second bell had rung, and it had surely been at least ten minutes. No one else seemed to be restless, though. At least not like me, unable to keep my excited—and probably nervous—energy in check, my fingers tapping on my thigh. Even the mysterious Andrés Mierza seemed perfectly at ease, content to watch and wait.

The red-haired woman caught my eye, smirking as she looked me over from head to toe in the way of predator sizing up prey. Her smirk deepened as she noticed my attention.

They knew. Somehow, they knew I was different. They always seemed to know. I'd barely even been at the Guild for ten minutes and they already knew. I was sure of it. And here I'd thought people wouldn't notice or care when I got away from my farm. I bit my lip, forcing my hands to still, my expression smoothing into practised neutrality. I pulled back from Windcatcher and Andrés, who was watching the other woman with a slight frown. He opened his mouth to say something—to the woman or to me, I didn't know—but before he could, four Couriers walked out from the white stone building of the hall and onto the field.

Thank goodness.

"Good morning, recruits," the eldest said, a man of about sixty, his grey hair braided over one shoulder, a patch on his shoulder indicating he was in the administration branch of the Guild. The three stripes beneath the patch had me forgetting my awkwardness of a moment ago. He was a Guild leader.

He controlled my fate.

The three other couriers carried two small tables and a writing desk, soon neatly set up so that assignments could be written down and given. I watched them intently, heart in my throat. Too intently, it would seem.

"Are you alright, Kayleigh?" Andrés asked, Windcatcher tilting her head.

I coughed and nodded, staring at the ground. "Just excited."

"Perfectly understanda—"

Thud. Thud. Thud.

Wind stirred up the field, whipping my braid through the air and making some of the other recruits shield their eyes. The Guild leader just sighed and held down the stack of paper that he had been sifting through, not bothering to look up. The sky darkened for a moment, then several shadows appeared and descended.

Courier dragons.

They were nearly twice the size of the draft horses that Papi kept on the farm for heavy work. Lean, shaped with smooth lines and graceful curves, they had long wings that were designed to carry them great distances without strain. Their tails were twice their body length and had tufts of fur at the ends. Their scales gleamed in the morning light as though they'd been freshly polished. They were, in a word, magnificent.

Andrés' breath hitched beside me. I saw the gleam of eagerness, excitement in his eyes. Even I was not immune to the awe of seeing the graceful dragons descending.

A courier wearing blue leathers leaped off the back of a forest green dragon slightly larger than the others and with longer horns, striding over to the Guild leader. "Sorry I'm late," he said, pulling off his cap to reveal muddy blonde hair. I had never been a good judge of age, but I would have guessed he was in his forties, care-lines worn at the edges of his eyes.

"What are the dragons doing here? We haven't

been given assignments yet," I whispered to Andrés. He leaned in a little closer, but his eyes were watching the dragons.

"The courier dragons entering service have to choose their riders before any other assignments can be given out," he murmured. "They get first pick of the recruits."

"Punctuality is a virtue, Rider Markham," the Guild leader said to the courier dragon's rider. "But now that you're here, we might as well—"

Thud. Boom.

This time, the shadow that descended was enough to blot out the sun as it rose over the horizon. It was at least four times the size of the other dragons, wings wide and powerful, scooping the air. There were gasps amongst the people on the field as they watched the dragon land.

My heart leapt into my throat, though I wasn't sure if it was from awe or fear.

The dragon was massive, built for power rather than speed, his midnight blue scales gleaming with a silvery hue. His horns were sharp, serrated, and he had spikes all down his back except for the hollow between his long neck and shoulders where a rider would be expected to sit. His tail whipped side to side, showing off the blade-like spikes at the tip. His claws dug furrows in the ground without effort and there was a heat to his breath that had steam rising from his nostrils.

That was not a courier dragon. Not a transport dragon, either, the larger cousins to the couriers who delivered parcels across Amontyr. No, this was a wardancer.

CHAPTER 2

"Apologies, Master Templeton," the terrifying dragon rumbled, inclining his head in a respectful nod. "I was unsure of where to be this morning."

"Seeing as you were only transferred two days ago to serve as a transport courier, I can understand the confusion," the Guild leader—Templeton—said, his expression twisting from alarm to forced calm. The bead of sweat on his brow belied the self-assurance he feigned.

Rider Markham clapped his hands together and his dragon snorted, adjusting her wings prettily. "Well, now that everyone's here, shall we get started?"

"By all means," Templeton said wryly. He

stepped forward and cleared his throat, pointedly turning his back on the wardancer. "Welcome, recruits. You have all been accepted into this noble and ancient chapter of the Guild of Messages, known to the world as Couriers. You are now responsible for delivering the post throughout the land of Amontyr, regardless of country or allegiance. You hold a sacred duty to see that messages and parcels get through, no matter the weather, the time, or the current political situation on the ground. Whether that be on foot here in Synval's illustrious capital city, Ilisar, or by dragonback to the far reaches of the continent. You are neutral, you take no sides. Your only duty is to the messages you bear. Welcome, and may you prosper here."

There was a smattering of applause, which I was a heartbeat late in joining. Andrés straightened, a smile of excitement touching the corners of his mouth. Even the red-haired woman seemed eager. All eyes, though, kept darting to the wardancer, his amber eyes fixed on the proceedings with a look of distinct boredom.

"Right!" Markham stepped forwards and his dragon joined him, lifting her head. "Before we get too far into divvying up assignments and sending you off to formal training, I ought to introduce myself. I am Rider Alistair Markham, and I am the training master for the Synval chapter of the Guild. We have training centres all over the continent, and you'll likely see many of them before you're ready to be sent off on your own. That is, *if* you are chosen to be a rider."

His dragon snaked her head forwards and nuzzled Markham before turning to the recruits. She shifted her wings, her green scales catching the light. "I am Guild Master Clover. Since I know your exams only covered the information lightly, I am going to go over it again. The dragons of the Guild of Messages are an elite group that serve all of Amontyr, unlike many of the other dragon services that are specific to each country."

Her eyes flicked to the larger wardancer, and she shifted, settling her forepaws neatly before her. "We are the ones who travel farthest and in times of most dire need. Because our service is so significant, we are granted with the choice of rider."

Her head swung to the red-haired woman, who immediately blanched and gulped, backing up slightly. "You have a question, Recruit?"

"Anna Talbot, Lady Clover," the woman said, voice quavering.

The forest-green dragon sniffed. "The proper

address for me is *Courier* Clover. A different status altogether. Certainly I have no idea why one would choose to be merely a lord or lady, but I digress. Your question, Recruit Talbot?"

"I-I heard that dragons take riders for life...?" Anna said carefully.

Clover snorted and pulled back, chortling. Markham stepped forwards and smiled gently at Anna, who was now flushing a bright red. The dragon spoke, "Most dragons do tend to work with their riders until they retire, but they can request a change if they feel the partnership is not suitable. Other services pair soulbonds, but the couriers do not—"

The wardancer growled out a single, sustained note, causing everyone on the field to freeze.

He lowered his head so that one amber eye was level with Clover's head. She rustled her wings again, this time obviously uncomfortable. I tried to remain as still as possible so as not to draw attention, but my hands were aching with the need to tap my fingers against my leg, to let loose some of the nerves bundled within me.

I wouldn't have to deal with dragons but rarely, I told myself. I was going to be a runner. A runner in Ilisar. I just needed to get through this morning and my formal training could begin. Yet my eyes would not leave the wardancer.

"Very well. My apologies. Courier-bred dragons do not take soulbonds," Clover said. The massive wardancer pulled his head back and went back to watching the proceedings with lidded eyes, looking bored once more. "Neither do transport dragons, mostly. Other breeds and backgrounds may be different. All of this will be covered in more detail if you are to join the rider service."

I suppressed a shudder, though if it was from excitement or fear, I didn't know. Even Andrés seemed a little nervous, watching the massive dragon carefully. Windcatcher hid her head beneath his hair.

"Anyways," Clover said, flapping her wings a little, drawing everyone's attention, "the dragons are going to choose their riders and then the rest of you will receive your assignments. And for those of you who joined the Guild purely to have a chance at being a rider, there is no guarantee of such things, so put the notion from your mind right now. We dragons have our own criteria for choosing our riders. Criteria we do not share."

Andrés cleared his throat and stared pointedly

ahead, gaze blank. Several others, including Anna, did the same.

With a flick of her tail, Clover's introduction was done. The dragons immediately started padding forwards, sniffing and examining the potential recruits with care. They didn't seem to ask any questions, only poking their noses into the recruits' chests or ignoring them completely. A seafoam green dragon with darker mottled green spots over her scales approached Andrés and me.

I remained stock still, my eyes cast down. Andrés's breath hitched as the delicate dragon nudged his shoulder. Windcatcher flared her wings and bobbed her head.

"Oh, I do beg your pardon!" the dragon exclaimed, drawing back. She blinked her bright green eyes and tilted her head. "You already have a dragon companion?"

"Since she was an egg," Andrés said, his voice edged with awe and confusion. "This is Windcatcher. She's nonverbal. I am Andrés Mierza."

"And I am Pennytyne. As you are obviously capable of caring for a dragon, then you may care for me as well. You shall be my rider." With that declaration, she settled down into a crouch at Andrés's side. Windcatcher fluttered to Pennytyne's muzzle, peering up at the larger dragon.

I stepped aside, throat tight. I wasn't sure why I was suddenly jittery, unnerved. Andrés was tending to Pennytyne, rubbing a spot just behind her jaw while Windcatcher perched between her horns. He seemed pleased with the dainty dragon, though there was a hardness to his jaw and a set to his shoulders that had some other emotion in them. Maybe it was his unknown emotion that had me on edge.

I was once again invisible. The other couriers were all busy with the dragons, trying to catch their attention or staying far away in an obvious show of wanting to be assigned as anything other than a rider. No one payed me any mind, just like always. That was alright. I wasn't here to make friends, though I knew that was what my family had hoped. I was here to be a—

"Where are you running to, Little Bird?"

I froze, coming face to face with a blue-scaled foreleg tipped with vicious claws. I tilted my head, only to find the massive wardancer peering down at me with hard eyes. My voice deserted me.

"Afraid, are you?" the dragon asked, snaking his

head down towards me, his massive wings spreading as if to encage me.

"Yes," I whispered.

"Honest, even in the face of fear. How unusual." He snorted hot breath that smelled of woodsmoke into my face. I flinched. "Don't be afraid, Little Bird. I will not harm you. *You* will be my rider."

Panic erupted behind my eyes. "You don't want me!" I blurted.

The dragon tilted his massive head, his horns catching the light. He seemed...amused? I gulped. "Oh? And why not? Those others are fools. They stare at me with covetous eyes, obviously here only for the prestige of being a rider. The others lie and preen and bow, pretending to be interested when really they tremble. You, though, you are honest in your fear. A brave trait. So you will be my rider. What is your name, Little Bird?"

"Kayleigh Espinosa," I said automatically. The wardancer nodded, as if it was something he had expected.

"I am Zapyros."

Zapyros. I tried to smile even as my heart raced. It was done. As Clover had said, the dragons chose their riders based on their own criteria. I was now a dragon rider. My dreams crumbled before me like ash on the wind.

CHAPTER 3

"You're making a mistake," I whispered, fingers tapping on my thigh though I tried desperately to be still. Zapyros was across the field at the bank of the river, drinking water and conversing with Clover and Pennytyne. Clover lifted her chin at something Zapyros said. Some of the other dragons were lounging in the sun or talking to their new riders. Andrés was gathered with a small group, including Anna Talbot, obviously thrilled with their fortune for the day. Windcatcher zoomed through the air around his head. His eyes kept shifting to me, to Zapyros, and I was fairly certain that he was frowning. I was left alone.

I was often left alone. It was just how I liked it.

"No, that's too rude," I muttered to myself. I was

trying to come up with a good way of telling Zapyros that he'd chosen the wrong person, that I was a terrible choice of rider. That I didn't actually want this. Nothing sounded right.

My stomach was in knots and I was quickly becoming overwhelmed. The rest of the courier recruits not chosen by dragons were being handed their assignments and ushered off the grass. That was where I was supposed to be. That I wasn't being led off was unnerving. Enough to make the world around me too loud, too bright, too much.

The world was always too much.

I was going to explode if I didn't get out of there. I needed to feel the steady beat of my feet on the ground, or, barring that, a dark room and the heavy weight of my blankets.

I wrung my hands together tight enough to hurt, but only a little.

"You are upset."

I yelped and jumped, startled to find Zapyros beside me as though he'd appeared out of nowhere. "Don't sneak up on me!" I snapped.

The dragon reared his head back. "I did not—"

I huffed and turned my back, the nervous energy and overstimulation building too much. I tapped my fingers against my thigh to the pulse of my breath.

Coherent thoughts fled my mind until there was only the tapping and the breathing.

Suddenly, the world seemed to darken around me and the noises became muffled. I paused, blinking my eyes at the change. Zapyros had folded his massive wings around me like a tent, sheltering me from the light and noise and from view of the others.

"You are Fey Spirited, aren't you?" he asked in a low rumble. "What they sometimes call a Changeling?"

I nodded, suddenly still. I sank to the ground and pulled my knees to my chest, wrapping my arms as tightly around them as I could. The pressure was comforting. Zapyros settled into a crouch, his wings pressing closer. A place of safety.

I'd known I was not normal my whole life. The world that everyone else seemed to enjoy was too loud for me. I saw too much, heard too much. Adults had conversed with me at their level when I was a girl, yet I could barely decipher the basic rules of society and so preferred to be on my own. When I was in company, I seemed to say the wrong things, or speak too little. People told me I was aloof. Intelligent but cold. Unsettling, even.

Fey Spirited. Changeling. The name they gave to

those whose brains were different. Abnormal. As though one of the ancient mythological Fey inhabited a human body. The term came from ancient stories about the times when the Fey supposedly still walked among us. They would exchange their sick children for human ones, leaving the ill child to be cared for by human parents, generally considered more nurturing. For the humans, though, it meant that one day their sweet human child became an entirely different creature. Sometimes they screamed at the touch of fabric, or they saw patterns in things no one had seen before. They were geniuses, or they were locked in a world of their own, unwilling or unable to communicate normally.

It manifested differently in each person, but for me, it meant that I was perceived as cold, harsh, aloof, unwanted by society and unable to understand why. I was intelligent, incredibly so according to the physicians, but couldn't understand the subtleties of social interactions. So I fell in love with maps and dreams of chasing them instead. There were stories of other lands where Changelings were still abandoned in the forests to be returned home, but thankfully Synval was above such things. "I've worked so hard to be normal, to be able to live a normal life. All I wanted was to be a courier, a runner, and now—"

"And now I've upset all your plans," Zapyros said. He sighed and adjusted his wings slightly so that a tiny slip of sunlight entered the space. Just enough for me to see Master Templeton hand out a final assignment. "If you truly desire it, I will release you from being my rider. You could still be a runner."

I nearly lurched forwards, despite being on the ground. "You would do that?" I breathed. Hope. This day could still go as I planned. I could still have everything I wanted. "Is it because I'm..."

"Fey Spirited?" Zapyros snorted, digging a claw into the ground and pulling up the earth. "I care nothing about such things. No dragon does, not when it is as common amongst us as it is with you humans. I picked you because you are honest and strong enough to run nearly three miles in twenty minutes. I saw you coming into town as I was flying here."

I started, then flushed. "You saw that?" I wasn't sure whether I should be pleased or embarrassed. Instead, I studied the ground. Zapyros moved his wing more, revealing the other couriers packing up the papers on the table.

"If you wish to make a change, do it now. Other-wise…" Zapyros flicked his tail, the blades on the end gouging into the ground. He huffed.

"What will happen to you?" I asked, even as I stood. I wanted to do nothing more than turn my back on the dragon and take my place as a runner. The thing I had wanted for as long as I could know such things. Zapyros remained silent.

"Zapyros?" I prompted. The dragon lifted his chin and let out a long breath, a hint of smoke flit-ting away on the wind.

"I am not like the other courier dragons," he said at last. "I transferred here after the treaty of Casper Venir was ratified. My previous rider…Wardancers bond for life, unlike courier dragons. And once the soulbond is made, no matter how short a time has happened, there is only one way to break it."

Meaning his previous rider had died. My heart ached for him, enough so that I put a hand on his scaled forelimb. The scales were smooth, only the edges sharp, and surprisingly warm. "And now I'm your rider? But we haven't even known each other for an hour and—"

"And? Am I not discerning enough to know my own mind?" Zapyros snorted and stood, shaking off my arm and rising to his full, massive height. "Go. Be a runner, as you desire. I will be fine."

I shifted my weight again. Indecision tore through me like a knife. But when I turned to go to the Guild leader, to tell of the change in my circumstances, I found I couldn't lift my feet.

"Maybe..." I said carefully. "Maybe there will still be running wherever we go."

Zapyros stilled, only the very tip of his tail twitching like an oversized cat. "Very likely," he said, just as carefully.

"And I'd still be a courier." My voice was more sure. The weight of my decision settled in my bones and I knew it would be difficult, but it was the right thing to do. For Zapyros, who had chosen me out of all the potential recruits, strange as that thought might be. And for me, too. I was sure of it, though I didn't know why.

"Indeed. A transport courier, no less, likely to see all of Amontyr," Zapyros agreed. He moved closer to me, lowering his head to peer at me with his amber eyes. I touched one of the smaller horns on his jaw and flinched at the sharpness.

"Then I think I'd like to be your rider."

Zapyros smiled, just a fraction, showing his

fangs. I shivered at the sight of so many impossibly sharp teeth in close proximity. But I smiled, too. Only a little.

CHAPTER 4

The other couriers exited the field in short order, off to train for their respective tasks, leaving the various riders and their dragons milling about, waiting. Part of me wanted to go with them, but I had given my word and I was oddly excited. I stayed where I was. Zapyros remained crouched by my side, his tail curled about me protectively. The other dragons gathered closer.

Clover reared back onto her hind legs and let out a screeching cry. Markham grinned at the new riders.

"Well, well, a good bunch of recruits, I think! Now, most courier training takes a couple of weeks, but you lot are in for the long haul. Not only do you have to learn the routes and protocol regarding long-distance couriering, but you have to learn how to care for your dragons and to ride. That is, to fly."

In a bound, Markham was on Clover's back, settling into the divot between her neck and shoulders. "Today you ride without a saddle to solidify the trust between you and your dragon. Don't worry, we'll go slow and I'll make sure no one falls off. Then we'll get you fitted out with courier leathers and measure you dragons for saddles. Okay? Great. Take to the skies, everyone!"

"Shouldn't you teach us how to hold on? Or the basic principles of flying? Or something?" Anna Talbot had her hand on the shoulder of her red dragon, but her eyes were wide and panicked. Andrés, I was surprised to note, looked equally worried, though it only showed in the thin line of his mouth. He looked to me and I quickly shifted my eyes to the ground.

Markham leaned forwards on Clover's back. "I prefer to throw you into the deep end. Sink or swim, riders. Let's go!"

With a flap of her wings, Clover leapt into the air and was aloft, heading towards the clouds with seemingly little effort. I gaped after the pair.

"Up you get, then," Zapyros grumbled. He grabbed me in his talons and lifted me to his shoulder. I squeaked as I landed on his rough scales, narrowly avoiding one of the sharp spurs of horn that ran down his back. "Settle into the spot in front of my wings. There's a divot—yes, that's it."

I crouched down in the natural impression between neck and shoulders. Given Zapyros's size, it was big enough for three men to lay side by side and still have room. The scales there were also smaller, smoother, with no rough edges that would cut me. It was almost comfortable, if one forgot about the fact that I was on the back of a dragon with deadly spikes and claws who could also breathe fire.

"Hold on!"

"Hold on to what?" I asked, but it was too late. Zapyros crouched and sprang into the air. The ground fell away and my stomach rose into my throat. Gasping, I squeezed my eyes shut. Each beat of Zapyros's wings made my heart race, and I held on as best I could, scrabbling for purchase on the smooth hide.

I was going to fall. I was going to fall and my career as a courier would be over before it began. My mother would say, "I told you so," at my funeral and my father would cry over my grave. My sister would probably take my room for her children before the day was out and—

"Open your eyes, Little Bird," Zapyros chuckled. I shook my head adamantly. "I swear upon the goddess Amarati, I will not let you fall. I will *never* let you fall. Open your eyes."

I took two deep breaths, then opened my eyes. Zapyros had levelled off, his great wings spread wide to catch the wind, making it seem as though he floated. Around us, the young courier dragons flew, their long wings twisting and turning as they cavorted through the air, showing off for their new riders. We were high enough that the sun glinted off of the dragons' scales, making it seem like a thousand jewels filled the air. And below—

I sucked in a breath. "It's like one of my maps," I breathed. The world stretched below me like a great map drawn in exquisite colour and detail. Roads that I had memorised on paper now lay before me in real life, painted in shades of brown and grey. There was the edge of the city, the meeting of the two rivers, and the plains beyond. The buildings were perfectly shaped, as no hand could possibly capture them, and if I looked closely, I could see the tiny dots that were people and dragons and animals going about their lives.

It was indescribably beautiful. My eyes welled. I brought my hands to my mouth to keep from sobbing. All my life, I'd poured over maps, wanting nothing more than to trace them with my steps. But this? This was infinitely better.

I wished that I could paint, draw. That I could capture the map below me with my own hand. I swore that I would get supplies at the earliest opportunity.

"Alright, everyone, back down to the ground." Clover winged by, eyeing the riders. I hadn't paid much attention to the others, too preoccupied with my own terror and then wonder. Now, I looked. Several of the riders were clutching their dragons with white-knuckled hands, though they were all able to rest their legs on either side of their dragons' necks for purchase, unlike me and Zapyros. Anna was whispering with her red dragon, making him laugh. And Pennytyne was flying lazy circles through the air, Windcatcher fluttering around her head while Andrés held on, wearing a fierce smile.

"Brace yourself," Zapyros said, but before I could ask what he meant, he snapped his wings in and plummeted. I let out a cry of alarm and instinctively ducked down, pressing myself as flat to his back as I could. The wind snatched at my hair, my thin clothes, and the ground sped towards us too fast. My stomach roiled, and I was grateful that I hadn't had a chance to eat anything that morning.

"Wardancer!" Clover shrieked, diving beside Zapyros. Markham leaned close to her back, watching with concern. "Pull up!"

Zapyros snorted, a single spurt of flame licking the sky, but a moment later he extended his wings and we stopped falling with a lurch. I groaned, squeezing my eyes shut again. Flying was going to take some getting used to.

"Are you crazy?" Markham shouted over the wind. "Land! Now!"

Zapyros growled, low and deep. Clover let out a startled hiss and backwinged away. The wardancer did land, however, coming to a gentle rest on the ground, his wings folded neatly and his tail twitching. He didn't offer to let me down, and he was far too tall for me to jump. I crouched on his back uncertainly.

Clover slid to a landing just in front of Zapyros, her wings half-extended, scales bristling. Markham jumped off her back. He looked so small from the great height of Zapyros's back. "You could have killed your rider flying like that without a saddle!"

"I would not have let her fall," Zapyros said with a toss of his head. "I am not so foolish as that. She was always perfectly safe. *Always*."

Clover hissed again, this time rattling her scales in an obvious threat. "You are not at Caspar Venir, wardancer. You are a *courier*, which means you are under *my* command. What you did just now may have been tolerated amongst the war mongers to weed out those you considered weak, but we value life here. All life, but *especially* our riders!"

Zapyros puffed out his chest and extended his wings, nearly blotting out the sun over Clover. "I told you, I would not have let her fall. She is *my* rider. I don't know what rumours and stories you listen to, but we wardancers fight to protect life, not to end it."

Markham approached, hands raised. "Let's all take a breath, alright? It's obvious that we just have a bit of a misunderstanding here. A different way of doing things. Right?"

Zapyros snorted but said nothing. He did, however, fold his wings. Clover did the same, lifting her chin.

"Courier...are you alright?" Markham looked at

me and I flushed to realise he didn't know my name. Out of everything that was happening around me, the arguing and the posturing, that detail seemed the most significant. The man who was supposed to train me to be a courier hadn't even learned my name. Had he learned any of the others' names?

"I'm fine," I said, not meeting Markham's gaze. "I trust Zapyros."

Markham nodded once, watching my dragon rather than me. He seemed disconcerted still, despite my reassurances. Zapyros, though, settled a bit, some of the tension leaving his shoulders. "Maybe you could let her down, then?"

He snorted, but complied, crouching down and extending a leg so I could climb down. Once I was on the ground, Markham looked me over as though checking for any signs of deception. I stared resolutely at his chin, not quite ready to see what he thought of me and yet too annoyed to fully look away, to show I could be so easily cowed.

I never was much good with respecting blind authority.

Clover shifted her wings and minced a few steps away, obviously some sort of signal because the other courier dragons started landing, looking over their riders and ignoring Zapyros completely. He huffed.

"Hey, are you alright?" Andrés wandered over, Pennytyne dogging his footsteps. Windcatcher leaped from Andrés's shoulder to fly about Zapyros's head, eventually landing on one of his great horns and looking a bit like a butterfly on a horse. A very dangerous horse.

"I'm fine," I said again. Andrés frowned. "Why does no one believe me?"

"Because you just about plummeted to the ground at a breakneck speed?" Andrés held up his hands as Zapyros blew a stream of smoke towards him. "I don't mean any offence, only it's a stupidly dangerous manoeuvre without a saddle, even *with* training. My father says that it takes years for trainees to be able to do something like that, and, well—"

"Your father?" Anna had wandered closer, her steps haughty and her chin high. Her dragon was at her shoulder; he puffed up his chest as they drew nearer to Zapyros, despite being barely a quarter of the wardancer's size. "Does he have much experience with the Aerial Corps?"

The soldiers and their fighting dragons. Where

Zapyros had just transferred from. I turned to Andrés, trying to hide my interest.

Andrés stiffened, suddenly taciturn. Aloof. "I could not say," he murmured.

"I'm Anna by the way," she said with a toss of her hair and a smile. "Anna Talbot, rider to Cyneric." The red dragon spread his wings and angled his head so that the sun caught his scales, nearly blinding me. I blinked and murmured a greeting, rubbing my eyes.

"Andrés Mierza, keeper of Windcatcher and rider of Pennytyne." He bowed formally. Windcatcher flapped her wings on Zapyros's horn and Pennytyne inclined her head gracefully.

"Er, Kayleigh Espinosa. And this is Zapyros," I said, gesturing to the wardancer.

"Zapyros?" Anna blinked, taking a step back. "But you're—"

Zapyros growled slightly. "I am a member of the Courier Guild now."

"The Guild of Messages," I corrected automatically. When everyone stared at me, I hunched my shoulders. "It's the Guild of Messages, officially. I mean, I know that people call it the Courier Guild, but it was originally established as the Guild of Messages by—"

"So, what do we do now?" Anna interrupted, ignoring me completely. I smoothed out my expression into one that was calm and relaxed, hiding the sting. I'd been through this before, this posturing and social jockeying that made so little sense to me. I could pretend to be like everyone else for a while, no matter how exhausting, how much it hurt to pretend.

"Now, we get you all measured up for riding leathers and saddles," Markham said, striding over to them from where he'd been conferring with Clover. He lifted his head to Zapyros. "Your transfer papers stated that you already have a saddle?"

"I have," Zapyros said stiffly.

"Good. Go fetch it, please. We'll leave it with the leather crafters to modify so it will be fit for courier service." Markham dismissed Zapyros with a wave of his hand. The wardancer didn't move. Clover hissed over her rider's shoulder.

"Do as you are bid," she snapped, showing her fangs.

Zapyros lowered his head so one great eye was in line with mine. "I will return."

I frowned, drawing my brow together. "I know." Why was he telling me?

He snorted and drew back, then leaped into the

air with a single bound, his wings snapping open. A few flaps had him disappearing from view.

"I know the situation is a bit unusual," Markham said, immediately turning to me once Zapyros was out of sight. "But we do need him. Our last transport dragon just retired and they are staggeringly rare across Amontyr. It's a bit difficult, him being bred for fighting and all, but we've had special provisions and certain allowances are being made so that everything is still in accordance with the neutrality of the Guild."

"I don't understand," I said. Markham pulled a hand through his hair and exchanged a look with Clover.

"We need you to cooperate with him as best you can. We'll transfer you as soon as we're able to find another dragon, but for right now, we need you to stick with Zapyros through training, at least." Markham looked apologetic.

"I'm his rider," I said, frowning more. "Of course I'll stick with him."

Despite the relief that painted Markham's features, I felt like I was missing something. That feeling persisted as I watched the other riders and dragons look at each other, exchanging glances full of meaning that I missed entirely. Clover and

Markham turned to go greet the leather crafters that had entered the field, and Anna and Cyneric went to be first in line for measuring. Pennytyne followed after, tail twitching eagerly. Andrés tossed a piercing look over his shoulder.

"It'll be alright," he said in a low voice. "I'll keep an eye out for you."

I just nodded, trying to smile, skin tingling at the thought. I slipped into line and wondered just why I would need to be watched. Why they were so worried about Zapyros. There was something else going on here, I was sure of it, but I didn't have enough information to unpack all the answers. Not to mention dealing with the intense stares from the mysterious Andrés. I would bet a month's pay that there was a great deal he wasn't saying.

As promised, Zapyros did return with his saddle clutched in his talons. The other riders gave me a wide berth, casting wary glances at my dragon as he delivered his saddle to the gaping leather crafters. The rest of the day was spent on the ground, small talk filling the empty spaces between riders and dragons as we were poked and prodded and measured for flight leathers and saddles. Still, by the time the sun started sinking towards dusk, I was as exhausted as if I'd run the annual twenty-mile race around Ilisar.

"Take these," Markham called, handing out a stack of books to each rider. "Read them by the end of the week. Now, go home and get some sleep. Tomorrow we start the hard work!"

He frowned in my direction then shook his head, mounting Clover and flying away from the field. He was not the only one who watched. Andrés studied me from where he stood by Pennytyne's shoulder, brushing away some dirt from her scales. When he met my gaze, he looked away as if he hadn't been watching at all.

I cradled the books in my arm, staring blankly at the covers.

"Do you want me to fly you home? My den is not far from where I saw you running this morning." Zapyros wound his tail around us in a protective circle.

"I think I'm going to walk," I said. "It's been a long day. I have a lot to think about."

Zapyros narrowed his eyes, but eventually nodded. "I understand."

He took to the air again, the beating of his wing ruffling my hair. I watched him until he was a speck in the darkening sky, then turned towards home. My feet ached too much to run and my mind swam with everything that had happened. I dragged my legs on the walk home, one that seemed impossibly longer than every other time I'd made the trek. My thoughts became nothing but noise until all I could do was focus on taking one step after another and holding the books in my arms.

That, and ignoring the speck that followed me in the sky, seeing me safely home.

CHAPTER 5

I had, in the course of the tumultuous day, forgotten one very important thing. So significant that I began to panic a bit upon reaching my family's farm. My panic had turned into my fingers drumming against the spines of the books in my arms by the time I reached the door of my house. I tried to focus on the little details, the single-story house of stucco and tile, the wooden beams that added a bit of coastlander flare to the design—my father's influence—and the flowers that bloomed, swaying in the wind.

All of it fell away as I opened the door.

"Congratulations!" The shouts filled the air. I jumped, nearly dropping my books. My parents, my grandparents, my sister and her two children, and my sister's husband, Marco, were there. Dressed in nice, clean clothes. Smiling. At me.

My stomach dropped.

"Come on, child, don't dawdle," my mother said, waving everyone else aside. "Go change and then come out to dinner. Your grandmother made your favourite. Go go!"

Before I'd even had a chance to blink, I was bustled back to my room. I dropped my books on my bed and automatically started changing into a dress that had been laid out for me by my mother. Like I was still a child.

My eyes welled, and I wanted nothing more than to give in and collapse onto the bed and pretend that the rest of the world didn't exist. But one descent into anxiety and panic was more than enough for the day, and my family was out there waiting. They'd dressed up. Carmen and Marco had even bothered to make an appearance, meaning that they actually cared. They actually marked the date. What did it matter if I was exhausted? They'd put forth the effort, so I would, too.

I took a little extra time to myself by redoing my braid as tightly as I could. I turned my back on my reflection in the bathroom mirror, humming tune-lessly to myself.

What were they going to say?

Mami would scold. She always scolded. My grandmother would just shake her head and dismiss it as another one of my eccentricities. Another way my life would never be normal. My grandfather would say nothing, as usual, likely more focused on his food than anyone else. Carmen and Marco would side with my mother. Papi, though, what would he think?

I didn't know.

"Dinner is getting cold!" Carmen knocked on the door to my bedroom twice, despite the fact that it had no lock. "Come out. We went to all this trouble. The least you could do is be prompt."

I opened the door and smoothed my skirt, not meeting my sister's gaze. "I'm here," I said in a low voice. Carmen looked me over and sniffed, but thankfully made no criticism, instead turning on her heel and heading back to the dining room.

The family was already seated, not having waited for me. Food was being served and conversation was well in motion. I found my usual chair at the end by my grandfather, my sister sitting across from me.

"Cows are a bit testy," my grandfather said,

nodding at Marco two seats down. "Calving season is a bit late this year."

"It's because of the dry weather," Marco said solemnly. "We need a good rain to get things started."

"No talk of cows at dinner!" Gran snapped. Granda had the grace to look abashed. "We are celebrating Kayleigh's venturing into the adult world. Tell us about your day. Do you have a district? Oh! The central district, no? You memorised all those maps, they surely placed you in the best district."

The central district had been interesting to me, full of well-off houses and courts and businesses that would surely need lots of messages sent. I took too long to respond, though, and my mother broke in.

"Ah, yes! You will be with the beautiful people and their beautiful streets. No running around in dark, dingy places." Mami didn't really approve of Ilisar. She was daughter of a wealthy dairy farmer and didn't like the city much. Unless it was high society, that is. Then she approved mightily.

"Er—"

"Did you see anybody famous?" Carmen asked, eyes bright and eager. She had married an aspiring dairy farmer, a good, steady man, but her heart always longed for the excitement of the city. A point of great contention between her and Mami.

"Actually, I didn't—"

"Plenty of time for famous people. Now she needs to make a name for herself as a reliable courier. People reward reliability," Gran said with a fervent nod. "If you are to be independent, then you will need to be reliable."

"Hush." My father's single soft word brought the table to a halt. "Let her speak. Kayleigh, love, how was your day?"

He smiled at me with those green eyes of his, so at odds with the brown of the rest of the family. His hair, too, was different. Blonde, though it was streaked with silver now. He had fallen in love with the plains and their spirited people, moving from his family home on the coast to marry my mother. It was a romantic story, one I had always loved hearing him tell. I had always wanted to do right by him, to keep from disappointing him, and now I was going to ruin everything.

There was no changing it, though.

"I'm not a runner," I said, looking away from his interested gaze.

I heard Carmen suck in a gasp. The rest of the table was heavy with silence.

"What do you mean, precisely, that you're not a runner?" Mami asked, her words slow and measured. Too slow. Too measured. If I lifted my head, I was sure to see panic written plainly on my mother's face. "Did you, ah, not get the job? Because of, well..."

"I still work for the Guild," I said. The rest of the words came out in a rush. "Only, they had the dragons choose their riders first before they handed out the other assignments and Igotpickedtobeat-ransportrider."

Marco coughed. "I'm sorry, you got picked to be what?"

"I'm a rider." I squeezed my hands together in my lap. "I'm a rider for a courier transport dragon."

I didn't add that this particular dragon happened to have transferred from the Aerial Corps and was a wardancer. I was honest, blunt even, not stupid. There were some things my family didn't need to know yet. I had found that unexpected news worked best in small doses.

The table was still silent. The seconds slid by and still no one said anything. The wait was interminable, almost painful for me. I lifted my head and found that everyone was staring at me. Well, everyone except Granda, who was busy stealing a roll out from under Carmen's nose.

"You can't be a rider," my mother said at last. It was a knife through my chest. "It's too dangerous. I mean, you being a courier—a *runner*—was one thing. Ilisar is so close and if anything went wrong then you would be close to home and we have some influence here to smooth over any ruffled feathers. But a *rider*?! No. You cannot."

"I am a rider, though," I said, frowning. "Zapyros chose me. It's not something that can be undone."

Mami laughed nervously. "It can always be undone! If they won't transfer you, then you'll just have to quit. You can't stay."

"It's not that dangerous. Couriers are neutral across the entirety of Amontyr. I won't be targeted for anything. Besides, Zapyros—"

"I don't care if couriers are neutral, you are not capable of it!" My mother's voice became a shrill cry. I blinked and recoiled into my chair. The rest of the table pointedly did not look at me, a twist from the norm. Carmen even went so far as to excuse herself to go check on her children at the small table in the corner of the dining room. Marco looked like he wanted to join her.

"I am Fey Spirited," I said in a low voice, trying to

hide my emotions. Anger. Hurt. Sadness. Desperation. I didn't know which it was, only that it was trying to choke me. "I'm Fey Spirited, but I'm not an idiot, Mami. All those teachers and all those tests say the opposite."

"It has nothing to do with how smart you are. The rest of the world isn't like the farm. People will treat you differently. You'll be stared at. You'll ruin any chances of a normal life with your...your...oddity." Mami was standing, now, her hands planted on the table, glaring at me.

"My oddity?" The world was spinning too fast. My mother had always been a bit exasperated with me. A bit strict, a bit sharp, but she'd never said anything like this before. She'd never talked to me as if I were *other*. "My brain is different, that's all."

"Yes, and the rest of the world isn't made for people like you."

I shot to my feet, the chair scraping on the stone floor, loud enough that I flinched. I wanted to say something, anything, in defence of myself, but the words wouldn't come. None of my masks that I had worn over the years—calm, confident, curious, capable, normal—had words for this. Instead, I just tripped away from the table, nearly knocking the chair over in the process, and ran to my room. I wanted to lock the door, but it had been removed years ago.

My mother's doing, I recalled, for fear that I would hurt myself during a meltdown. I'd been seven. The lock had never been replaced.

Panicking, I cleared off the top of my dresser and pushed the heavy piece of furniture in front of the door, wincing at every scraping sound. Moments later, the door rattled and then slammed. Voices were on the other side. Mami. Marco. He was probably the one who had tried to break it open. Carmen. Gran.

I was breathing too heavily. I couldn't catch my breath and my eyes were full of tears. I wanted to curl up in my wardrobe or bathroom and cry myself empty, but the door kept slamming and the dresser started moving a bit. A bit more. More.

I grabbed a bag from the wardrobe and started shoving clothes into it. My box of money I'd saved over the years doing odd jobs for neighbouring farms. My new books. A second pair of shoes. I grabbed my courier uniform last of all and shoved it on top before slinging the bag over my shoulder and running to the window. It wouldn't be long before someone would think to check on me that way.

Thankfully, there was no one outside just yet. Only the dark garden illuminated by a half-moon.

I climbed out, closed the window behind me as best I could, and wincing at the crack of wood that said someone was trying to break the door entirely, ran into the garden. I minced my steps on the crushed stone so no one would hear, but once I reached the low stone wall that separated the house from pasture, I lengthened my stride and I ran.

I hadn't wanted to be a runner for nothing, after all.

I didn't know where I was going until I was already there, at the top of a hill where the herding dragon Grimble liked to nap during the day so he could watch the cattle herds without having to move from the shade of the trees. He wasn't there now, likely in his barn by the cattle sheds. It was perfect for me, though. There was an ancient oak tree with branches that were so thick with leaves it was impossible to see through them.

It also had a hollow near the roots that I had dug out into a small cave as a child. Back when I liked to pretend to be a pirate or a knight or someone that went on adventures. Before I fell in love with maps and the thought of tracing them with my own two feet.

The hollow was smaller than I remembered, a tighter squeeze now that I was an adult, but I fit and it was safe and quiet. I lay perfectly still for a few minutes, straining my ears past my racing heart. No one was coming. There were shouts in the distance, meaning they'd likely discovered I was gone, but they weren't following me. I was alone. I was safe.

Finally, I began to break down. It was trembles at first, and tears that I tried to wipe away. Soon the tears flowed too fast to catch them, so I buried my face in my knees and pressed my back deeper into the hollow.

I didn't know how long I lay curled up like that, crying, but eventually my tears dried and the shaking subsided. I knew I needed to figure out what was next, but I couldn't. All I could do was stare at the moonlight speckling the leaves.

"Kayleigh?"

I flinched. Held my breath. It was my father. And, judging by the crunch of his footsteps on the grass, he was alone.

"Are you out here?"

I unfolded myself from the hollow and stepped out, one hand on the trunk. "Papi?" I rasped, voice rough from crying. He turned towards me, hair gleaming bright in the moonlight. He smiled.

"I thought I'd find you out here. Grimble always said that this was a favourite haunt of yours, before you started running everywhere."

I said nothing. My father sighed and sat on the ground beneath the oak. He patted the spot next to him. I sat.

"What your mother said was ill put," Papi started. I stiffened. "She didn't mean it like that."

"She did." I was certain. I was many things, but I was not a fool. The words my mother spoke had been the truth as she saw them. "I think after so many years of dancing around me, my differences, she finally meant what she said."

Papi twisted his mouth. "I'm sorry." He wrapped an arm around me. I would normally have pulled away, since so many people's touches were half-hearted, light, unsettling things that made my skin crawl. I liked it when people put weight into their touch, but most didn't know how to do that. Right now, though, I sensed that this wasn't for me, but for my father.

"I can be a rider," I said quietly.

"Of course you can. You're an adult. You can make your own decisions. It's just...I thought you wanted to be a runner. Will you be happy as a rider?"

I considered. "I think so. I still get to be a courier. And I get to see the rest of the country. There will still be running involved when I get to my destinations. And I like Zapyros. He's like me."

"Oh?" My father raised his brows. I pulled away from his touch.

"Not Fey Spirited, but kind of on the outside of things. We went flying a bit today. Just a little bit. It was—" I paused, searching for the words to explain that nauseated, astonished feeling. "Breathtaking. It was like looking at a map of the world, only so much better. He showed me that. And he'll keep me safe."

Papi considered. He nodded. Took a breath and then nodded again. "It's not the life I would have expected for you, but if it's what you want, then you should do it."

Relief lightened the burden on my shoulders. "What about Mami? She tried to break down my door. She took my lock. She doesn't think I can…"

Papi sighed. "Running away from your problems won't fix them. But neither will confronting them when you're full of hurt, anger, full of pain. Take some time, yeah? Your Mami loves you, but she doesn't always see the person you've become. Instead, she sees what you were when you hid behind her apron strings. Be sad, Kayleigh. Be angry.

Be hurt. But don't forget that you are loved. No matter what."

"So what do I do?" I breathed. I was starting to cry again. This day had been far too emotional for my tastes. I had just wanted to run and deliver messages. Impersonal. Swift as the wind. Completely forgettable. Instead, I'd nearly broken down more than once. I hated crying. It was so messy. "Get a room in the city?"

"That would work. Give you a chance to spread your wings a bit. Besides, you have your own money, more so now that you're with the Guild."

I fidgeted with the grass beneath me, stripping the blades. "I've never lived on my own," I murmured. Maybe it was time that I did.

"But you know how to cook. How to clean. You like your space just so. Think of this as a chance to have your own space, just the way you like it. Besides, I'm sure some of the other riders will help you, if you need it. You can always come home, if you decide you don't like it. Always. Okay?"

I nodded and leaned once more into my father's arms. This time, he put extra effort into squeezing my shoulders, just the way I liked it. I nodded again. My heart still hurt—it likely would for a long time— but I had a way forward. I had a plan. I had Zapyros.

CHAPTER 6

My grand plans for finding lodgings in the city were far less grand with a crick in my back from sleeping on the hill. I had made arrangements with my father to send on the rest of my belongings once I had an address. Until then, he would work on my mother and I would hope that there was somewhere I could stay. Somewhere I could afford.

I did not run into Ilisar with the dawn, instead yawning my way past the watch dragons and pausing to spend a penny for some tea and a sweet currant bun to sate my hunger. I hadn't actually managed to eat any dinner the night before, after all.

The field outside the Guild hall was empty for all

of a moment before a shadow descended and Zapyros landed on the ground beside me as lightly as a cat. I jumped.

"You need bells or something!" I grumbled around a mouthful of bun. Zapyros flicked his tail and extended his nose, sniffing.

"You smell of grass and cows. And you have twigs in your hair. Did you sleep outside?" There was a definite air of disapproval in his voice. I shrugged. I wasn't about to delve into the complexities of my familial situation just yet. Thankfully, I was interrupted.

"Kayleigh!" Andrés jogged up, looking as though he'd already been on a run, his hair damp and his face glistening. Windcatcher soared beside him, twirling in a few circles around Zapyros's head before landing on his horns. "How are you?"

Maybe he could help me. I put on an expression of good-natured frustration, one I knew was sure to gain sympathy but not pity. "My housing situation fell through," I complained. "I have to find a new place to live. Immediately."

Zapyros narrowed his eyes at me, sniffing my hair again. He growled low and deep in his chest, startling Windcatcher. "Is this why you—"

"You wouldn't happen to know of a place I could

stay, would you?" I asked Andrés, tilting my head. He looked surprised, wary, casting a glance between me and my dragon. I ignored Zapyros completely. The last thing I needed was my dragon roaring his way to my family farm to scold my mother. That would only make things worse. Much worse.

Andrés pulled his brows together, concerned. "I could ask around, I suppose. But there's always—"

"Ask around for what?" Pennytyne alighted on the field with a delicate twitch of her wings. She blinked blearily at the group and yawned, showing off pointed fangs that gleamed in the rising sunlight.

"My rider has need of a place to stay," Zapyros said, obviously disapproving. He nudged me with his muzzle. Hard. "Her housing situation fell through."

Pennytyne settled with her tail wrapped around her legs like a cat. "Oh. Well that's simple enough. The Guild has rooms for its members. They like it when their people are close at hand in case a message needs to go out in the night. That's why most of the dragon dens are in that hill, there. Though they don't really have anything big enough for you." She eyed Zapyros.

"I will make a space," he declared. He nudged

me again, this time towards the entrance to the Guild. "You go get a room. I will sort out my den. It is better to have you nearby anyways. Safer."

"I'm not in any danger!" I protested, though I dutifully walked towards the hall. "I just need a place to live."

Zapyros snorted in response. Pennytyne lowered her head to Andrés.

"You could move here, too," she suggested, flaring her wings hopefully. "It would be good. In case there's a message, I mean."

Andrés laughed and scratched a spot under her chin. "I have a place to live, my dear. Better to save the rooms for those that need them."

I turned, hiding a smile. Dragons were apparently quite possessive over their riders. Even non-hoarding dragons like couriers. I wondered if wardancers were hoarding dragons. Grimble was, but he was meant to herd the cattle and considered them his hoard. Many watch dragons and herding dragons were the same way. I really should have read some of those books last night for information on wardancers, but it had been too dark under the oak tree. Tonight, I vowed.

I nearly ran into Anna emerging from the hall.

"Watch where you're going!" Anna snapped. She paused and frowned. "Oh. It's you."

"Morning, Anna," I said. "Um, sorry, I just need to get by and—"

"It's a mistake, you know." Anna folded her arms, glaring in the direction of the field where Zapyros and Pennytyne were talking with Andrés.

"What's a mistake?"

"Having a wardancer join the Guild. They're not peaceful dragons, everyone knows that. They can't be part of a neutral Guild." Anna wrinkled her nose as she turned back to me. "They'll realise it soon. He'll be transferred back to the Aerial Corp and then where will you be?"

I shifted my weight, not sure how to respond. I must have waited a beat too long to answer, because Anna just huffed and tossed her hair, leaving for the field without a backwards glance. Another weight seemed to settle on my shoulders. I wondered just how my life could have changed so much in the space of a day. And how much more it would change.

Inside the Guild hall, I quickly found a clerk to direct me to the quartermaster's office, where I filled out a housing form, was handed a key and map to my new rooms. Another map for my collection; I bit my lip to hide a grin. The quartermaster, a bored looking woman with silver hair and mahogany skin, looked me over twice before frowning.

"I'll show you where the rooms are," she said at last. "So you can put your bag away before work."

"Thank you," I said, relieved. "That's very kind of—"

"And while you're there, maybe you can comb out your hair. You have sticks in it. Couriers must maintain a well turned out image, for the good of the Guild."

"Oh. Right. Of course." I dropped my gaze to my feet, my hand reaching for my braid. I winced when I found a twig and a leaf, just as the quartermaster had said.

The lodgings for Guild members was across a courtyard near the hill where the dragons lived in their carved-out dens. They were simple enough quarters, consisting of a bedroom, a sitting room, a bathing chamber and a small kitchen. I was told that a portion of my pay would be deducted for the room, and if I wanted to deduct a few extra coins, I could have hot meals every evening in the dining hall. I quickly agreed. The quartermaster sniffed and nodded, then left me alone.

I dropped my bag near the bed. "I did it, Papi," I murmured. "I found my own place."

So why did I still feel like everything was topsy turvy?

CHAPTER 7

Training that day consisted of going over the courier's manual as well as the extra provisions regarding dragon riders. Most of the courier recruits were eager to settle in and discuss the finer points of being a courier, especially in regards to dragons, but I found myself bored. I had, after all, memorised the manual before my entrance exam. Even the parts about dragons.

"Neither weather nor political circumstance shall prevent the delivery of post, though delays are known to happen." Clover looked over the group of riders and dragons, her eyes settling on Zapyros for a beat longer than otherwise. "Couriers are not bound by politics and are therefore allowed to deliver the post regardless of country or political situation…"

I sat on the grass and leaned against Zapyros's broad side, enjoying the warmth from the fires within his belly. I supposed that all of this would be new to Zapyros, given that he had transferred from the Aerial Corps, which was as far removed from courier service as one could get. I wondered what parts of the Amontyr he had seen, if I would get to see any of the places he had been. I really should start keeping a log book of my own, to draw my own maps in and document the places I'd been. That would be infinitely better than reading about the makers of maps in the Ilisar library. Not to mention—

"Are we boring you, Rider Espinosa?" Markham asked in a sharp voice. I blinked, bringing my focus back to the training master. He was frowning at me. Well, at Zapyros, too, but mostly at me. I flushed. "Perhaps you would care to tell us what comes next?"

I ran through my knowledge of the manual. "'When a country's governance demands that the post be turned over to their control, it is within the rights of a courier to deny them and deliver the post to each recipient individually, bypassing the local service.'"

Clover snorted, shuffling her wings. Markham set his jaw. "Do you think you're above this information?"

I reared back. "What?"

"Do you enjoy making a mockery of being a courier?" Markham took a step forwards. Zapyros slid his tail around himself, creating a boundary between Markham and myself, the blades on the tip of his tail glinting in the sunlight. I shrank back.

"Wasn't that the answer?" I asked in a whisper. Silence met me. Markham exchanged a look with Clover, then snapped his book shut.

"Since Rider Espinosa here seems to think she doesn't need a thorough examination of the manual, then we're going to do something different and you all will have a written exam on the contents of the manual at the end of the week."

Zapyros growled, the sound barely audible except through the vibrations of his scales. The other riders groaned. Anna bared her teeth at me in a furious smile, her dragon Cyneric going so far as to hiss at me. Only Andrés said nothing, not even both-ering to look my way, busy with scratching Windcatcher under the chin. Somehow, being ignored was worse than the attention.

"Let's go!" Markham snapped. He stalked towards the edge of the field where the leather-workers had already started to set up their equipment. "Time to get those saddles fitted."

Now it was time for the dragons to groan. Zapyros sighed. "It was the right answer, Little Bird. I'm sure of it," he said to me, eyes fixed on Markham. "That one has something stuck in his teeth about me is all. I promise."

"Punishing one of us for the other, especially when we haven't done anything, isn't fair," I murmured. I rubbed a hand along the sharp spines that framed Zapyros's jaw, careful not to catch my fingers on the points. He was hardly suited for courier service. Anna was right. But that didn't mean the others had to punish him for it. He chose this, that should be enough for them.

"Life is hardly fair," Zapyros replied. He bared his fangs as Markham pointed at us, gesturing to the leatherworkers. I tapped his leg.

"Don't antagonise them. You'll only make it worse," I whispered. Zapyros huffed, but complied, walking towards the leather crafters who had his saddle out. They were obviously regularly assigned to the courier Guild, their usual leather crafting Guild patches coupled with the courier stamp. Though when faced with a massive wardancer who was already in a bad mood, they blanched.

"Riders, you're going to learn how to saddle your dragon. Most of these saddles can be put on and taken off by your dragon alone, but you'll still need to know how to make sure the saddle is in good repair, whether it needs to be adjusted or replaced. Thank Rider Espinosa that you're now spending the rest of the day on saddle maintenance. And once we're done with that, you can go over your dragons and check their scales for mites or dry patches." Markham lifted his chin and the riders once again grumbled as if on cue.

Andrés and Pennytyne approached the leather-workers next to Zapyros. "Why is Markham so bent on alienating you?" Andrés asked under his breath, careful not to look directly at me. I shrugged.

"Because of me," Zapyros said, perfectly audible to the entire line. "He wishes to make it difficult on her so that she will transfer, forcing me out of duty since I won't take another rider. Such was the implication of our conversation at my den last night."

Everyone paused, wide eyes shifting between the training master and the wardancer. Anna even gaped at Zapyros, a frown forming when she looked back at Markham. Clover danced her head from side to side, wings flaring. Markham went red, fuming.

"Ah, you thought I would keep that conversation to myself?" Zapyros asked, voice almost a purr. "That I was afraid of what you would do to my rider if I revealed such information? She is stronger than you give her credit for, and she has done nothing wrong. Nor, for that matter, have I."

"Zapyros, hold your tongue!" Clover hissed, showing her teeth. Zapyros chuckled, smoke rising from his mouth. He said nothing further, only turning to face the leather crafters.

"Well?" he asked them. "Are you going to test the saddle or not?"

Andrés chuckled, catching my eye with a knowing smile. I quickly looked away. What had I gotten myself into?

The field quickly became a hotbed of activity, riders and leatherworkers scurrying around and on top of the dragons. Most hadn't already had a saddle made up, so they were spending a great deal of time on fittings and adjustments. Zapyros had a saddle already, only requiring modifications for courier work, so I only had to learn how to put it on and take it off. Or, well, unfasten it so Zapyros could take it off himself.

The piece was massive, made out of thick ox hide and reinforced with steel at some of the more crucial junctions. Zapyros put it on by snaking his head through the straps and shrugging it on with his shoulders. There were slots underneath, I realised, that fit over some of the spikes on his back so that their points were high above the leather. There were straps that wound across his chest and between his front legs, as well as a second set that secured beneath his belly behind where his wings connected. It was segmented so that he could bend and twist without restriction. Once the thing was on, it looked like he was wearing a large set of plate armour.

Perfect for a combat dragon, I decided, though it looked a bit heavy for a courier.

The rider's seat was in that same divot behind his neck, a moulded section that would let me ride for hours without fatigue in my legs, or ride laying flat if I so chose. When Zapyros picked me up and set me on the leather, my breath hitched. It was worn smooth from someone else's use.

His previous rider.

"Do you see the courier modifications?" Zapyros

asked, twisting his head. "It doesn't feel much different than it did."

"There are pouches along the side," I said, walking down the length of the saddle. "Also straps and clips for larger cargo. Some oilcloth in case we need to protect things from the rain. Is it comfortable?"

Zapyros stretched, catlike, then flared his wings, nearly knocking over one of the leatherworkers. This earned a hiss from Clover, which he ignored. "It feels much the same. The belly straps are thicker, and the front buckle rubs. What about your seat? Is it comfortable?"

I winced. I didn't want to take the seat of a dead person. But Zapyros was already twisting his head around, so I sat. The leather was hard, unforgiving, but if I relaxed into it, it was steady, secure. I straddled his spine easily, my legs held nicely in the divots formed there.

"It's comfortable," I said, running my hands over the smooth leather. My fingers caught on a rough spot and I froze. There, carved into the leather, was a name. Obviously done by human hands, it was small and crude. Zapyros would never have seen it. Only his rider. I traced the letters.

Garret.

"Who was Garret?" I asked, then immediately wished I hadn't. "I'm sorry, it's none of my business. I didn't mean—"

"Hush, Little Bird," Zapyros said, though there was a hint of a growl to his voice. "It's alright. I wouldn't be here if he hadn't..."

My words were barely a whisper. "You don't have to tell me. I understand."

Zapyros lowered his head. "Perhaps it is too soon. Another time."

"Are you two going to keep chitchatting, or are you going to get on with your task?" Markham walked up, his hands folded behind his back, his expression completely blank. I stiffened. I had thought him a somewhat reasonable person the day before, someone I could work with while being trained as a courier. Now, though, he seemed like nothing more than an angry man with an agenda.

"Well?" he asked. Fire bloomed beneath my skin, as bright as the sparks that Zapyros blew on occasion. I longed to lay into the training master, to demand that we be treated fairly. But I knew from experience that saying those thoughts out loud only made things worse. Often much worse.

I was not naturally inclined to conflict, preferring quiet and peace over arguments. I enjoyed following rules; they put a firm path in place for me to trace. Yet I knew that Markham's authority here was being misused. Despite the fire that tickled my spine, I knew that it would end poorly for Zapyros and myself if I spoke. So instead, I started tugging at buckles, tightening them and loosening them. Zapyros, thankfully, said nothing more, only lowering me to the ground so I could fiddle with the other straps. The saddle itself was too big for me to manage on my own, but I could fasten the straps. So I did.

Over and over and over again.

While the other dragons got their saddles fitted properly, their riders helping to measure and cut and tighten, talking happily with their dragons, Zapyros and I put on his saddle then removed it. Again and again and again. And by some mutual agreement, we said nothing more to each other, filling the air with tense silence every time that Clover or Markham approached.

By late afternoon, Zapyros was fidgety with unexpressed anger. Sparks kept leaping from his breath, landing on the grass and having to be stomped out. The tip of his tail twitched, slicing through the plants of the field until there was a clearly mown spot where his tail passed. The leather crafters had long since abandoned us to their own devices after adjusting the front buckle, the saddle otherwise perfectly adequate.

Finally, Markham called an end to the day's session, reminding everyone to study their manuals for the written exam. Riders and dragons alike scattered faster than I could have imagined. Andrés lingered for a moment with Pennytyne and Windcatcher, smiling gently at the pair as they played. He looked up at me as if just noticing me.

"Do you want to go find something to eat?" he asked, taking a step closer. His arm twitched as if he was going to raise it, to brush at my cheek, my hair, something, but he held himself still. "Myself and a few others are getting together at the river wharf for the start of the summer fish fry."

The first fish fry of the season was almost a festival in Ilisar, full of food and people and street performers, dragons, boats, games, even dancing when the drink flowed enough. It ran every night for a week and was a highlight of the year. "That would be—"

"Surely she has some studying to do?" Anna appeared, Cyneric at her side. She glared at me until I lowered my gaze. Andrés said nothing, his expression no longer warm, but carefully blank.

"I think I'm just going to have an early night," I said. "It's been a long day."

Anna snorted. She stepped closer to Andrés, resting her hand on his shoulder, murmuring something to him that I worked very hard not to hear. He nodded, then the two riders and their dragons left the field to go into town. Andrés looked back and Zapyros snorted sparks from where he lounged near the river's edge.

"You'll have to do better than that," he called. Andrés stiffened and nodded, then followed after Anna, Windcatcher flitting around him. I wrapped my arms around myself.

"Espinosa."

I whirled, finding myself face to face with Markham. "Sir?" I bit out. To my surprise, his expression softened.

"I know you think that I'm being unnecessarily harsh on you. But I can assure you that this is for your own good. To be rider to such a dragon—"

"For my own good?" I repeated the words, that earlier fire overriding my common sense. Markham, Anna, even Andrés. My mother. Everyone. I was tired of the rules demanding my silence in this matter. "Hardly."

"I beg your pardon?" Markham lifted his chin.

"That's what people like you—*normal* people— say to people like me when you want me to do what you say without question. It's what you say to people who are different when you want us under control." I scoffed. "I'm a courier. I passed the exam with the highest marks of this year's recruits. I answered your question correctly. I have broken no rules. Yet because I'm a rider to Zapyros, you think you should punish me. Or is it because I'm Fey Spirited that you don't like me? Either way, *sir*, I don't believe that you have my best interests at heart."

I didn't wait for an answer, taking my satisfaction from the horror that flickered in his eyes for a brief moment before I turned my back on him and stalked over to where Zapyros rested by the river, his body half-submerged in the water.

"Do you feel better, Little Bird?" he asked.

"Much."

"Even though you know that things will likely be more difficult for us?"

"Even then," I said. "I'm going to be the best damn courier he's ever seen that one day he'll have to pin the Medal of Messages on my chest."

Zapyros grinned at me, revealing every inch of his wickedly dangerous fangs. "Good," he said, and that was that.

CHAPTER 8

"Can you get this thing out of my teeth?" Zapyros practically pounced on me the next morning as I returned from a run. I was a great deal calmer for having spent the evening alone and going running, but having a massive dragon all but drop on you from the sky with no warning will set anyone's heart racing.

"Bells!" I said on a gasp. "You need bells!"

Zapyros answered by laying his head on the ground and opening his maw as wide as it would go. "Ifs ing da akc."

I looked at the many, many sharp teeth and sighed. All I'd wanted from life was to be a runner. To dash from one place to the next with no one bothering me on the way. To deliver messages. Now,

I was all but crawling into the mouth of a dragon, trying not to step on his tongue or get impaled by his fangs.

I saw the offending piece of bone—lamb, if I wasn't mistaken—stuck between two back molars and steadied myself on a fang while I fished it out, only to discover that the backs of Zapyros's teeth were, in fact, serrated. I cursed, blood welling on my palm and fire pulsing with each beat of my heart.

"Ooo okay?" Zapyros asked, tongue tasting the air.

"Fine." I pulled out the bone and crawled from the dragon's mouth, cradling my hand to my chest. It was bleeding everywhere, dripping on my clothes and Zapyros's mouth. He hissed, pulling back, practically throwing me on the ground.

Stars bloomed behind my eyes. Emotion most certainly not my own flooded my senses: shock, panic, confusion, then sheer determination. I couldn't see properly, couldn't hear, could only gasp under the onslaught of emotion and noise. A moment later and a wall seemed to slam down inside this new place in my mind. I lay there a few moments more, the world reasserting itself.

Grass, wet with dew beneath me, soaking into

my clothes. The sky too bright for all that it was barely after dawn. My hand, throbbing in pain.

"Are you alright?" This wasn't Zapyros who asked, but Andrés, appeared as if from nowhere, Windcatcher fluttering around his head.

"The soulbond has finally snapped into place is all. It took longer than I expected. It can be startling at first," Zapyros said, appearing in my field of view, amber eyes glinting.

"Oh, is that all?" I asked in a daze.

Andrés frowned. "Soulbond. Of course." He looked to Zapyros, who snorted. "Here, Kayleigh, let me help you."

I let myself be pulled upright, still cradling my hand to my chest. I looked at the shallow cut, which had already stopped bleeding. It was nothing more than a few clean lines, bright red and glistening, but not nearly as deep as I thought. Even as I stood there, staring, the lines seemed to disappear until they were nothing but smooth white scars.

"Um," was about all I managed before Andrés snatched my hand and stared at it.

"What happened?" he demanded, looking up to Zapyros, who reared back as if he'd been struck. I could sense something from behind that wall of stone in my head—anger, perhaps—but it wasn't clear enough for me to understand. Was I sensing Zapyros's emotions? Did that mean he could feel mine? I knew I should be more panicked about the cuts that vanished, but all I could bring myself to do was stare.

"Is there something inherently magical in dragon saliva?" I asked, twisting my hand in the light.

"It can happen sometimes, if a dragon accidentally injures their souldbonded," Zapyros muttered. His head wove back and forth and his tongue tasted the air nervously. "I didn't mean for you to get hurt."

"It's alright."

Andrés was still holding my hand, fingers warm against my skin. I pulled back, looking away. "Sorry," he said, taking a deliberate step back. Silence stretched between us for a beat too long, and I knew that it was going to turn awkward any moment now.

"Anyways, I'd better get changed into my uniform," I said, stepping around both Andrés and Zapyros and jogging towards the Guild Hall. Behind me, I heard a *thump* that sounded like Zapyros slamming his tail into the ground, but I ignored it.

The emotions pulsing weakly from behind that new wall in my mind I ignored also. Or, more accurately, I shied away, throwing up my own barrier on instinct. Only when I was inside, safely ensconced in my rooms, halfway out of my running clothes, did reality assert itself. I stared at the scars on my palm.

What had I gotten myself into?

"Today, we're going to be flying manoeuvres." Markham paced up and down the line of dragon rider recruits, studying each of them before moving onto the next pair of rider and dragon. He ignored me entirely. "You dragons are all young, too young to know the difficulties of flying with a rider for long periods of time. And you riders will have to learn how to fly, adjusting your grip and muscles so that you can move *with* your partner, not against it."

"Like riding a horse?" one of the recruits asked. He was older than most of us, a smattering of grey in his dark hair, though his black skin showed no wrinkles. His dragon, a red-and-silver mottled female snorted, tossing her head.

"I am not a horse!" she protested. Immediately, he lay a hand on her side.

"Of course not, Nalia," he soothed.

Clover shuffled her wings, the tip of her tail

twitching. "The principle is similar, though more complex given that we dragons are larger, stronger, and fly. For today, you will follow behind me. And you will do exactly as I tell you, no matter how bored you are or how well you think you can do it on your own."

Zapyros dug his claws into the soil, irritation bubbling over that wall. I flinched and the emotion immediately receded. "She means us," he whispered, though a whisper from him was loud enough to carry. Markham whipped his head around and narrowed his eyes, though he said nothing.

Maybe my words had gotten to him. Or maybe he was waiting for the right moment to make an example of me. Either way, I wouldn't give him the satisfaction of seeing me fail.

Clover gave the order for the riders to mount and, after a flurry of activity that was far from practised or graceful, everyone was in the saddle. I scrambled up Zapyros's extended leg, settling into the well-worn divot in the saddle, that carved name staring up at me.

"I am not a yearling dragon to be so cowed," Zapyros muttered, taking a bit of care to keep quiet. "Nor am I so small as a courier that a rider will strain me."

I lay a palm on the blue hide before me, marvelling at the warmth. "We are going to do exactly what they tell us," I cautioned. "If you don't...if *we* don't, we're going to get in trouble. And they won't throw you out, since you're the only transport dragon they've got, but me? I'm...expendable."

Zapyros let out a low snarl that set the stones on the ground to trembling. The courier dragons all looked at him in alarm, some even going so far as to jump away, wings flared. Only Andrés looked perfectly calm on Pennytyne, who rolled her eyes at the others. Windcatcher let out a screech.

"Is everything well?" Markham asked coldly.

"Very well," I said evenly, forcing my expression to be neutral, empty. He stared at me for a moment as if he expected me to crack, but I'd been wearing masks of emotion my whole life. To fit in, usually, but hiding how I felt wasn't new. Finally, he looked away, mouth tight. Points to me.

He patted Clover's side as he climbed into the saddle, then on a single beat, the two of them leaped into the sky. The other courier dragons rushed to follow, snipping at each other as they got in the way.

"Maintain order!" Clover snarled, wheeling about to face the unruly dragons. "You are not nestlings any longer. Cyneric, you take point. Nalia and Pennytyne, fall in behind them. Yes, that's better. A straight V-formation, if you please. Zapyros, why are you not in the air?"

With a sigh that produced sparks of fire, Zapyros extended his wings and leaped off the ground, a single beat taking us into the air. We dwarfed the other dragons, enough so that their formation faltered as the wardancer approached from behind. Finally, though, they settled and the entire band flew off after Clover.

Within five minutes, I could tell that Zapyros had been right. This was about as boring as flying could get. If one discounted the feeling of air on the skin, of seeing the world in tiny, expansive detail. We flew in circles around Ilisar, the courier dragons struggling to stay in formation as Clover constantly called after them, telling them to lift a wing or stop straining their necks. The riders, too, seemed to take a bit to adjust, constantly shifting in their saddles with the movement of the dragons' wings. Zapyros, though, flew with ease, his eyes half-lidded. It was as if he were hardly thinking, just blindly following after. And as for me, the saddle was stiff, but it wasn't uncomfortable, and it was large enough that I hardly had to work to keep myself seated, even given the leather straps holding me in place.

"Still determined to do as you are told?" Zapyros asked on our third circuit around the city. Clover had fallen out of the lead position and was now checking in with each rider and dragon, making sure they were flying properly. Andrés and Pennytyne seemed most at ease, but though Andrés rode as if he'd been doing it his whole life, Pennytyne seemed to struggle a bit carrying her rider.

"We have to," I replied. Clover came back to us and flew circles around us, Markham watching carefully. She got too close to Zapyros's right wing, and he blew sparks at her. She squawked in indignation.

"What do you think you're doing?" Markham snapped.

"Maintaining a safe distance from other dragons while flying in formation," Zapyros said, his voice smooth and dull, as mine had been earlier. But he *was* a dragon and couldn't help but add, "*Sir.*"

Markham curled his lip. He murmured something to Clover, who tossed her head and flew off, glaring back at us.

Zapyros hummed. "You may have a point. That was deeply satisfying."

"It's useful for subverting authority without actually contradicting them," I agreed. "But it isn't going to be much help for learning new things.

Flying in circles isn't going to teach me about being a rider."

"These...exercises are meant for the yearlings, not for us. But I have been flying nine years and you are not so foolish as to fall off on a simple dive." There was a hint of pride in his voice that made me wonder if that glorious dive on our first ride had been a test. I frowned. "We shall simply have to practise more advanced techniques on our own."

"Okay," I blindly agreed, still thinking. Then, "Wait, what?"

"Simple. Come to the field after supper and we shall train on our own." Zapyros shrugged his shoulders, which, in midair, was like riding a boat through the rapids on the river. I held tighter to the saddle, clenching my legs. "We will do proper flying."

I hesitated. I wanted to be done with this day, to get back to my new rooms and settle in. To read. To try and come to terms with my new life. But I also hated shying away from a challenge. "Fine."

"Bank left!" Clover called. Apparently we were done flying in circles and were now going to practise banking. The courier dragons did so, some of them baring their teeth against the strain of flying with a rider. Zapyros just sighed and followed along. Bored again.

For the next few hours, we flew basic turns, sometimes landing for a brief break and then leaping back into the sky as soon as Clover deemed us rested. Zapyros and I gave up talking to each other as Markham and Clover seemed to fly by us on a regular basis, often getting too close for comfort. Zapyros did his best to ignore them, but I saw more than a few sparks fly from his mouth when they got too close.

Irritation bubbled up over that new wall in my mind, and for once I didn't shrink away, sharing in the emotion fully. By the time Markham and Clover called an end to the day's session, I was ready to snarl at anyone who got too close. Instead, I kept my face a careful mask of neutrality and unbuckled Zapyros's saddle, checked his scales for dry spots and mites as instructed—though he protested this, muttering that he was perfectly capable of looking after his own hide—and finally started for the Guild Hall when we were released.

"Hey, Kayleigh!" Andrés jogged up beside me, Windcatcher riding his shoulder. "What did you think of flying?"

"It was nice."

Andrés frowned. Even Windcatcher blinked, tilting her head at me. "Nice? Is that all?"

I shrugged. Markham and Clover were still on the field, talking to one another and occasionally casting glances at Zapyros, who was nodding at something Pennytyne said, her wings flared with excitement. "It would have been better if we could have really flown, not just followed in circles."

Andrés chuckled weakly, rubbing the back of his neck. "Yeah. It does seem silly for them to have you doing the same thing as the smaller dragons. I mean, Zapyros doesn't need to worry about flying with a rider since he's done it before. And since he's, well, you know. Massive. You probably feel like a feather to him."

"Yeah. Probably." I waited a beat, decided he wasn't going to say anything further, then started again for the Guild Hall.

"Wait!" Andrés called. I paused. "Um, do you... do you want to go to the fish fry tonight?"

I spotted Anna and some of the others already heading in the direction of the riverfront. They weren't paying attention to me, but that didn't stop me from imagining the things they might say behind my back. "Maybe another time. I've got plans with Zapyros after supper."

"Don't hurry back on my account." Zapyros was suddenly there, his head hanging over my shoulder. I jumped and glared.

"Bells," I mouthed. He flashed his fangs at me in a smile.

"Go to the fish fry," he said. "I fancy a bit of fish myself."

"Do, uh, you want to come, Zapyros?" Andrés asked, staring at my dragon with unusual intensity. Zapyros considered, but the tip of his tail was starting to twitch and there was a hint of eagerness flowing over the top of that mental wall. He did.

"Come on, then," I said, waving my hand. "We'd better go before we miss all the performances."

CHAPTER 9

The streets and buildings of Ilisar were made with the needs of both humans and dragons in mind. During festivals like the fish fry, though, things were almost unbearably crowded for me. Dragons of all sizes wandered through, sometimes flying from one spot to another, and while they were generally careful, there was always the chance of getting hit by a wing or tail as they moved.

Or, well, that was what had happened when I'd attended festivals in the past. Walking through the festival with Zapyros directly behind me an entirely different experience. He was the largest dragon in the city by far; even the watch dragons only came up to his chest. Everyone moved out of his way, leaving me plenty of space. Even having Andrés and Pennytyne right beside me didn't make me feel claustrophobic.

The relief at such a boon was palpable.

"Let's get something to eat first, alright?" Andrés said, pointing to a line of booths right by the river. The fishermen and dragons delivered their catch directly to the food booths, who were frying and sauteing, grilling, baking, and so much more. The scents were myriad and tantalising.

"Fried fish! Get your fried fish!" The owner of the booth practically shoved a basket of fried fillets in front of my nose. I recoiled.

"Hmm." Zapyros lowered his head and sniffed. "Garlic?"

"And oregano." The man pulled back the human-sized portion and eyed Zapyros eagerly, already reaching for the largest cut of fish he had. "Served with a side of potatoes and roasted carrots."

Zapyros's tongue snaked out, testing the air. "I'll take two."

He pressed his right front foot onto the ledger as an indication of payment. The booth owner would take his ledgers to the bank and the funds would be pulled directly out of Zapyros's account. Some dragons carried money—mostly the smaller ones— but most did not.

"I'm going to get some baked fish from over there." I indicated the booth being run by a woman moving with the efficiency of a master, ignoring the shouts and squeals of excitement up and down the street.

"I think I'll join you," Andrés said. "Pennytyne? Do you want some?"

The little courier dragon was sniffing the meal being prepared for Zapyros. Already several other dragons were starting to gather. Apparently what was good for the massive wardancer was good for them, too. She ignored Andrés in favour of crouching to watch the food being prepared. Windcatcher landed on her head and watched, too. Andrés shrugged, and we moved off.

He was polite enough to wait until we had our meals before starting to ask questions. "It seems you and Zapyros are creating quite a stir with our mentor."

"You mean Markham and Clover don't like me." I took a careful bite of the fish and sucked in a breath. Hot!

Andrés winced. "I, ah, wouldn't have put it like that."

"Why not? It's true." My second bite was easier to manage. I realised after I had already taken it that I should probably put some of my attention on Andrés instead of staring at my food. I lifted my eyes and found him frowning at me. I quickly went back to staring at my food.

"You haven't done anything, though. You've gone through all their exercises, haven't complained, know all the answers to their questions..." Andrés grumbled and took a bite of his own food. I chuckled. It was amusing to see him upset on my behalf. A rare enough occurrence.

"Zapyros is different. A wardancer. Not bred to courier life. And I'm different. They certainly didn't expect a Changeling to be placed with a wardancer. Two different people together? They think it's a problem." I shrugged and looked at Andrés again. He was gaping at me, but as soon as our eyes met, he winced and closed his mouth.

"Sorry. I just...you're a Changeling? Fey Spirited. Sorry. That's the more polite term. I just...Sorry."

I snorted. "No need to apologise. It doesn't matter what you call me. And yes, I am. Markham doesn't know what to do with me. Or Zapyros. So he doesn't like me. I've been dealing with this sort of thing my whole life."

Andrés winced again. He reached out and lay a hand on mine. "You shouldn't have to deal with any of that," he said softly.

My cheeks heated and I couldn't quite bring myself to look away, even though actively meeting his gaze was making my stomach squirm and my heart race. After a minute, Andrés coughed and pulled back, taking another bite of food.

What was that? I finished off my own dinner and ran through what little I knew of the subtleties of human interaction in my brain. The only thing I came up with was ridiculous, because no one bothered to flirt with me. Ever.

I shifted my weight and looked longingly back towards the Guild Hall.

"Are you done eating, Little Bird?" Zapyros asked, appearing once again like a cat out of the shadows. His tongue darted out to clean the scales on his muzzle, showing off a massive fang. Several people in the vicinity of the food booths moved away. "There are games to show prowess and skill over there. You should try some."

"What?" I stared at him. "No. I don't need to—"

"You are skilled. You should prove it. Then there will be no one who dares to argue against you." Zapyros said this with a casual twitch of his wings, as though such overt scheming was something everyone did, every day.

"I don't need to *prove* anything," I snapped.

"Not to yourself, no, nor to me," Zapyros said, sniffing. "But to them? To those fools who claim to train us?"

"They're not even here!" I glared at my dragon, hands on my hips.

"Come on, Kayleigh," Andrés said, laughing. "Let's just go play some games, okay? There's no arguing with a dragon when they're like this."

I kept glaring at Zapyros for a moment, but there was something smug in his expression that had me wanting to play just to prove to *him* that I wasn't someone who could be ordered around. It made no sense, and I knew that, but somehow Andrés was pulling me away from the food and towards a large circle where simple games where set up.

There weren't any large enough for Zapyros to play, and most dragons preferred to test their skills in areas of flight or fighting or in testing their wits against other dragons, so he settled into a relaxed crouch at the edge of the crowd and watched, eyes mostly closed, as if he wasn't even paying attention. He even had the audacity to yawn.

"Why that ridiculous, infuriating dragon!" I hissed. "What does he think he's doing?"

Andrés grabbed my hand and pulled me to a booth set up for slingshots. "He thinks he's getting you to have fun. To participate in the festival events, even if he has to goad you into it. Or were you not planning on going back to the Guild Hall directly after eating?"

I hunched my shoulders. "How did you know that?"

"Because that's what you did last night. You don't seem to like crowds of people much. More comfortable on your own?" Andrés paid a couple of coins to provide us with a slingshot and three bean bags each. I weighed mine in my hand and grumbled. I hated that I was so easy to read.

"It's okay to enjoy being alone," Andrés said, nudging me with his shoulder. "But sometimes people can be fun, too."

I looked back at Zapyros, who smirked at me.

"Fine."

Andrés grinned, and we stepped up to the game, slingshots at the ready. The person running things was a short man with a leering grin. He looked me over once and immediately turned his attention to Andrés. "If you can knock the target over with one of your bags, then you can win any prize you like. Perhaps a present for your partner?"

Andrés flushed, the dusky colour on his cheeks highlighted in the torchlight. "Er, um, we're not..." He looked at me wide-eyed.

If this was meant to be fun, then I obviously wasn't meant for fun. I lifted my slingshot and loaded one of the bags, raised it and fired. The target —a small brass circle at the end of a range—fell over. The gamemaster gaped at me. Feeling petty, I loaded the second bag and knocked another target over. And the third. I practically threw the slingshot down and scowled at the man.

"What skill!" he said, voice shaking a bit. "Claim your prize."

I pointed to a stuffed toy in the shape of a dog made to look like a real hound, large enough to stand at hip height. It was ridiculous and absurd, but it was better than the gold bangles or creepy doll. I carried it in my arms over to Zapyros, who was laying with his head on the ground, half-asleep.

He jerked when I set the toy down in front of him. "Proof," I said.

"What?" The genuine confusion in his tone, and the way he curled a lip at people trying to get too close to me, had me feeling bad. Maybe he was just trying to get me to have fun. It wasn't his fault I was in a bad mood. I was just adjusting to the fact that being a courier wasn't anything like what I had hoped. What I had dreamed.

I pushed the toy closer. "I won it for you."

Zapyros brought his snout close to the toy, staring at it with wonder. It was tiny compared to the massive dragon, but he picked it up with care, cradling it in his forepaws. "For me?"

I felt even worse now that he seemed to really like the toy. "For you," I agreed.

"Thank you." He sat back on his haunches, holding the toy close. When Andrés approached, looking chagrined and without a prize, Zapyros held out the dog. "Look what my rider won for me!"

Pennytyne lifted her head and sniffed. "It looks soft! Andrés, will you win one for me?"

His flush deepened. "Oh, er...I'm not as good at that game as Kayleigh. Maybe I can win something at a different game?"

Pennytyne and Windcatcher immediately set off to go investigate the various games and determine which one Andrés should try next. He shot me a chagrined look. "Where did you learn to do that?"

"My family's dairy farm. Grimble, the herding dragon, told me that if I was going to be running around everywhere, I might as well make myself useful and learn how to keep the vultures and coyotes away during calving season." It was the only time of year he really tolerated me.

"Well, now you have to help me win something for Pennytyne and Windcatcher, or I'll never hear the end of it." With that, he grabbed my arm and dragged me off, leaving Zapyros to sit and watch with his new toy, showing it off to the other dragons gathering around.

CHAPTER 10

Andrés departed the festival apologising profusely to Pennytyne and Windcatcher while I followed along behind with Zapyros still holding his toy.

"I'll buy you a present to make up for it," Andrés said. Pennytyne sniffed and lifted her head, refolding her wings on her back.

"It's not the same," she insisted, twitching the tip of her tail. "You did not win it."

"I earned the money," Andrés begged. "Isn't that the same thing?"

Pennytyne turned her head away. "No."

Andrés turned to me with a pleading look. I tried not to laugh. He hadn't won a single game. He hadn't even come close. I'd offered to win something at the slingshot game again, but apparently it wasn't the same. Windcatcher finally settled on his shoulder and rubbed her head against his cheek, obviously forgiving his abysmal performance at the festival games. Pennytyne watched this interaction with a sour look.

"Will it be a big present?" The young courier dragon studied the toy Zapyros had settled carefully on his back so it would not fall. He turned to look at it every few moments, nudging it into place when the movement of our walking had shifted it.

"I promise," Andrés said. "Big."

"But not too big," Pennytyne said. She twisted her head around to study her own back. "I have to be able to carry it while flying with you. And I like shiny things. But I don't think a stuffed toy would look right made of shiny fabric like silk."

"I'll bring you a ring for your horns. Would that suit?" Andrés asked, almost desperately. Pennytyne considered, then nodded and lowered her head. Andrés kissed her forehead gently, scratching her chin. "Now go on. It's getting late and we still have to be up early tomorrow."

Pennytyne chirped, threw one last jealous look at Zapyros, and leaped into the sky.

"We, too, have to be going," Zapyros said imperiously, the tip of his tail twitching eagerly. "Come, Kayleigh."

I waved goodbye to Andrés, too worn out to say much. There had been too many people, but the festival *was* fun. Not that I would admit as much to Zapyros and his smug expression.

We went back to the Guild Hall, and I was sorely tempted to suggest we start extra training the next night. Unfortunately, Zapyros was as dogged as anticipated. He held his toy in his talons and crouched down.

"What, no saddle?" I started climbing up, already expecting a refusal.

"You did perfectly well flying without a saddle our first day. Saddles are for security, for long distances, for carrying things. Training without one will improve your skills. Hold on." With that unhelpful warning, he leaped into the sky. I cursed under my breath and settled into the divot on his shoulders, hands splayed on his hide while he climbed higher and higher.

By the time he levelled out, Ilisar was a collection of shimmering lights below us. It was too dark to make out any detail, and I found that I missed the view. Still, the flying was stunning. The air was crisp, the wind in my hair almost like running.

"Are you settled?" Zapyros asked.

"Yes."

"Good." With that, he folded his wings against his side and fell into a dive. I cursed much louder this time. Because of his size, it was difficult to hold on with my knees like I would on a horse or smaller dragon. I tried laying flat, but the wind tore at my clothes and tried lifting me away from his back, so I lunged forwards and grabbed at one of the pointed spikes, holding on to that instead. I found that if I braced myself against it with my shoulder and wrapped an arm around it that I could hold on quite easily and was in less danger of being impaled when he finally pulled out of the dive with a casual swoop.

"You could have warned me!" I snarled.

Zapyros turned his head to grin at me, showing all his teeth. "What would be the fun in that? You figured it out, didn't you?"

I had. And while that was somewhat satisfying, I still scowled at him. Zapyros laughed and kept flying.

For the next hour or so, we flew. Zapyros didn't talk much, but then, talking to him was far more difficult when battling against the rush of wind in my ears. This was nothing like the gentle formation flying we'd done earlier that day, where there was no screaming wind, no holding on with muscles I wasn't sure I had a few minutes ago. It was much, much better.

Zapyros flew up at steep angles, diving and twisting, turning on a whim and then catching himself on his sail-wide wings to jerk to a stop midair. He rolled over, tucking his wings in tight, and then flew in a loop so quickly that I didn't even have time to protest, though I did—loudly—when he pulled out of that particular manoeuvre, my legs dangling in midair and my fingers screaming as I held on. By the time he landed gently on the ground, I was trembling from exhaustion. My arms ached. My jaw hurt from clenching my teeth against some of the more terrifying movements. My legs wobbled.

But I had held on for everything.

"Well done," Zapyros said, pride bubbling over that wall in my head. I pulled away from the emotion and shrugged, wincing at the movement. Zapyros nosed me, amber eyes narrowing. "You are sore."

"Of course I'm sore!" I lifted my arms and groaned.

"Those were simple, straightforward manoeuvres. You should not be sore. We will just have to practise more."

"Or you could communicate before you fall out of the sky." I harrumphed, kicking the ground. Then, I considered. "How do riders communicate with their dragons when the wind is too loud?"

Zapyros settled his wings on his back. "Some riders tap out messages on their dragon's back in a sort of code. My hide is too thick to feel much unless you pound, though, so I would not recommend that." He looked around as if expecting someone else to be there, watching, listening. Then he moved closer. "For us, you could just reach through the soulbond. I will hear you wherever you are."

"That wall in my mind?"

"Yes."

"How?" I certainly wasn't going to shout at it.

"Just...close your eyes."

I did as I was asked, thinking of the wall. It was as detailed as an actual wall, a closing of a part of my mind that I knew didn't truly belong to me alone. Mentally, I reached out and touched it and was surprised to feel stone as though I were actually touching the stone wall surrounding Ilisar. Only, with my hand on the wall, I could feel Zapyros's emotions much more clearly. Curiosity. Excitement. Contended peace after exertion.

"Good. Now, keep touching the wall. Think

something at me, like you would were you speaking."

I ran through a myriad of options, trying to come up with a scrap of poetry that I'd memorised or something at least somewhat profound to say. It seemed silly to just think, *"Hello,"* at the wall, but then I never was very clever at coming up with profound responses on the spot.

"Hello to you, Little Bird." Zapyros's voice rang through my thoughts. I yelped and pulled back from the wall. He laughed, the sound a rough growl. "I think that's enough for one night. Go. Sleep. We will practise more tomorrow while we do whatever idiotic task Markham and Clover come up with for us."

I nodded absently, still shivering. "Goodnight, Zapyros."

"Goodnight, Little Bird. Sleep well."

With a single shake of his wings, he was in flight, and though I couldn't see his midnight blue form against the blackness of the sky, I had no doubt that he circled until I went into the Guild Hall.

CHAPTER 11

For the next few days, Zapyros and I came to a silent agreement. During the day, we would comply with all the ridiculous requests that Markham and Clover threw our way. We flew in formation at a ridiculously slow pace. We practised loading the saddle with makeshift packages for transport and then flying with that (the other courier dragons practised with small bags of letters and small parcels). We stood there while they inspected our equipment, Markham alternately pretending to be overly nice to me, or—when my stone-faced mask irritated him too much—snappish and sharp.

But in the evenings, we flew.

Sometimes with the saddle, but more often

without, Zapyros and I took to the skies. Sometimes we practised the more difficult manoeuvres, twisting and twining through the sky like a fish through water. My muscles were still aching, but I could tell that they were getting stronger. Other times, though, we just flew, taking in the land as the sun set and swallowed the world below into darkness. I purchased a set of drawing supplies and a notebook in town and started practising drawing my own maps of the places we flew. I was terrible, but there was something wonderful in creating a map of my own.

Documenting my explorations of the world.

Every morning, I still ran, and while I enjoyed it just as much as I ever had, I found I preferred flying. Just me and Zapyros and the wind. It was a sort of magic I'd never experienced before and I loved it.

Then came the day of the promised examination on the courier manual that Markham had assigned. Instead of going out to the field to meet with our dragons, we were ushered inside the Guild Hall to an empty room that had been set with desks and paper and pens.

"You have two hours," Markham said, pacing by my desk. He watched me for a moment, jaw tense. I returned his stare with an empty look. He turned away, the tips of his ears as red as the anger in his eyes. "Begin."

The exam was nothing special. I'd already memorised the courier's manual for my entrance exam into the Guild, so this was just a matter of repeating what I already knew. I wrote swiftly but precisely, forcing myself to be slower than the first person done with the exam. I knew from experience that people didn't like it when I was first done with a task. They wanted to see that something was as difficult for me as it was for them.

Markham, I imagined, would be no different.

So when two people had completed their papers and turned them in to him, I took up my own paper and set it on the desk, focusing my gaze over his shoulder.

"I only do this to ensure you are well prepared for courier work," Markham said in an undertone, taking my paper with care. I met his eyes—a challenge—and said nothing. "Your insubordination will earn you no favours."

"Insubordination?" It was difficult to keep the incredulity out of my voice. "Begging your pardon, sir, but in what way have I been insubordinate?"

"You..." He frowned. I had done everything he asked without complaint. Finally, he scowled and waved at me. "You just...stare! You don't say anything unless asked a question. And your face!"

His voice was rising in volume. I heard someone come up behind me. Andrés, now standing at my shoulder, set his paper on the desk. He raised his brows at me. Markham waved him on, but he didn't move.

"My face?" I asked, keeping my tone perfectly even. It was much harder to keep my anger in check and I had to fight to keep it from spilling against that wall in my mind. Zapyros could know nothing of this interaction. "I was unaware that the Courier Guild judged people on appearances."

Markham turned red. "It's not your appearance, it's your damned lack of expression! If you just behaved normally, then—"

"Sir," Andrés cut in, voice low. I put a hand on his arm and he closed his mouth. I pointed to the door. He gave me a lingering look, but he went. Then, I turned back to Markham.

My voice flat, I said, "I did not know that the Courier Guild required a person to display a wide range of facial features in order to be successful at their work. I appreciate you explaining such to me, given my inability to behave normally, as you said. I will endeavour to do better in the future."

Markham spluttered and tried to backtrack, but I simply smiled sweetly, making sure he knew the expression was forced, and left. Our encounter had been heard by everyone in the room; they all stared, some at me, some at Markham, but they all stared. I was used to the ridicule, the whispers, but I doubted very much that Markham was.

I did not look back.

"Eyes on your papers!" Markham roared as the door closed behind me.

"Kayleigh." Andrés leaned against a wall, obviously waiting for me. "Are you alright?"

I was furious. I shrugged. "Why wouldn't I be?"

"The things he said. Those were beyond the pale. I can't believe he would—"

"It's fine." I shrugged again, rubbing my breastbone with my hand to relieve the familiar ache there. "I'm used to it."

Andrés grabbed my wrist and turned me towards him. His eyes lidded, he licked his lips. On a rasp, he said, "You shouldn't have to be."

The ache in my chest was replaced with something deeper, much warmer. It spread like wildfire through my limbs and I was sure my face was going to combust with how warm it was. I bobbed my head in a nod, not sure what to say.

"I'm going to report Markham," Andrés said, finally releasing me. "What he did—"

"You will do no such thing!" I snapped. "I'm dealing with it." The door to the exam room swung open and Anna stepped out. She looked between us. I half expected her usual sneer, but she just looked upset.

"Hey, uh...That wasn't okay, you know that, right?"

I recoiled. "You would have me do *nothing* when he said those things?"

"No! That's not what I meant. I meant what he said, that's not okay. I can't believe he would...is he always like that with you?" Her voice was quiet, but not like she was trying to keep people from over-hearing. It was like she was ashamed.

"More or less, depending on witnesses. It's because of Zapyros. He doesn't want him here, and because I won't give him up, he tries to bully me instead." I frowned. "Why?"

"Because that's..." Anna shook her head. "He's our training master. He's supposed to help us. Support us. Not...You haven't done anything wrong. I mean, you're, well, odd, but that's no excuse. You know the manual back to front. You can handle your equipment better than anyone. You're the best flyer in the group, and not because your dragon knows what he's doing. Actually. Um. Would you, maybe, help Cyneric and me? With our flying?"

I blinked. "Oh." Then, because I didn't know what else to say, "I thought you didn't like me. Or Zapyros."

Anna flushed as red as her hair. "You certainly don't beat around the bush, do you?"

"Sorry. That was rude." I tried for a smile and ended up with something that I hoped wasn't a grimace. "But it's true, isn't it?"

Anna fidgeted a bit, looking to Andrés as though he would step in. When he didn't, she turned back to me. "I'm sorry. For the things I said to you. I thought...Well, I thought that having a wardancer in the ranks would upset things, would make it impossible to keep neutral, but Zapyros is the steadiest of all the dragons. They look up to him. Cyneric says he gave up fighting to be here. That means something, you know. That he chose this. Chose you."

A part of me wanted to turn away, to snub her like she'd snubbed me and see how she liked it. I knew it was petty, though, so I didn't. Instead, I took the apology for what it was. This time, my smile was more sincere. "I'd be happy to help you and Cyneric. You'll have to ask Zapyros, but he's a sucker for flattery and will probably see any request for help as acknowledgement of his superiority."

Anna chuckled. When I didn't join in, she burst out laughing. "You're serious!" She threw her arm over my shoulder and led me out to the doors to the outside, Andrés trailing behind looking bemused. "I think I misjudged you, Kayleigh. I think you and I are going to be great friends after all."

CHAPTER 12

Zapyros was dozing in the field, the very tip of his tail twitching when one of the smaller courier dragons got too close. They were all lounging together, waiting for their riders. Pennytyne kept tilting her head this way and that to make the silver ring on her right horn shine, but she had been showing off for a few days now and none of the other dragons seemed to care any longer. This only served to make her grumpy.

Windcatcher landed on Andrés's shoulder almost as soon as he stepped outside, burying her head in his hair and flipping her wings. She grumbled when Pennytyne appeared.

"You are done, now?" The light green dragon

shoved her snout towards Andrés, sniffing. "You smell like paper and ink."

"That is what an exam requires, dear one." Andrés scratched her chin.

"Well, now we can go do something. The others are boring, just lounging around and not talking about anything interesting." Pennytyne huffed, tossing her head in just the right way for her silver ring shine again. I hid a smile behind a cough.

Andrés patted her side indulgently. "Kayleigh has promised to help us learn how to fly better."

"I'll get Cyneric," Anna said, already jogging to meet her red dragon. Zapyros stretched as if on cue, his claws digging great furrows in the earth. He yawned, showing off his fangs.

"Now that you are done with your papers, we can go, yes?" he asked, lumbering towards us. Wind-catcher launched herself at him and perched on his head like a sentinel. Zapyros flicked his wings, waiting for me to climb onto his back. We'd been given the rest of the day off since the exam was to take up a good portion of our usable day and I doubted very much that anyone would be terribly cooperative afterwards.

"Anna and Andrés have asked for help with their flying," I said. Part of me wanted to relay what

Markham had said, but I doubted Zapyros would take such treatment quietly. He had taken quite well to pretending compliance, but I knew that his protective nature was of the act first variety.

Zapyros tilted his head towards me. "And you approve of this plan, Little Bird?"

"Sure," I said. "Why wouldn't I?"

Zapyros narrowed his eyes. I half expected him to say something about how the others had treated me, but he was silent. He just snorted and shrugged. "I'll go get the saddle, then."

In a bound, he was airborne, returning a few minutes later with his saddle in his claws and Windcatcher flying circles above him. Cyneric and Pennytyne were already waiting, the red courier dragon dancing with excitement. He shook his head, his scales rustling. "Finally we get to do proper flying. Those fools are holding us back."

Pennytyne twitched her tail and tossed her head to make her ring glint in the light. "They *are* our training masters," she said. "Perhaps—"

"Do you want to know how to fly in more than a straight line?" Cyneric snapped his teeth at her. Windcatcher hissed, flaring her wings.

"Maybe we should—" I was interrupted when a large man wearing an elaborately embroidered jacket wheezed his way through a jog towards us. He was holding something in his hand, waving it in the air. Behind him, a boy who looked like his son pulled a cart loaded down with crates.

"Courier!" the man said, stopping right in front of me. "Special delivery!"

I leaned back before he could accidentally hit me in the face with the missive. Andrés plucked it from the man and unfurled it, revealing a missive sealed with the blue-and-gold wax that indicated it was, in fact, a special delivery.

"Ten crates from Bartwell and Sons to be delivered to Hadrian Nadreth of Dun Kennis," Andrés read.

"Immediately!" the man—Bartwell, I assumed—snapped.

"We'd better find Markham," Anna murmured. Zapyros lowered his head over us, peering down at the missive. Bartwell squeaked and stumbled backwards, nearly falling into his cart.

"A wardancer!" he said, pointing at Zapyros.

"A transport dragon assigned to the Courier Guild," I snapped. "Or are you too blind to see the crest on his saddle."

Bartwell gaped at me, eyes flicking between Zapyros and myself. He apparently decided that scolding the rider of a wardancer was not the wisest course of action and snapped his mouth shut with an audible gulp.

"Your missive will be carried out," Zapyros said, though he rolled his eyes at the theatrics. "Kayleigh, help the lad load my saddle." With that, he crouched down, looking smug.

"We're only in training!" Anna protested, albeit quietly. I don't think Bartwell or his son were paying much attention, given that they were hemming and hawing over the cart and who would load it onto Zapyros's back.

"You're couriers, aren't you?" Zapyros asked, one large amber eye suddenly very close to the redheaded woman. She stilled. "You are bound to deliver when a missive is given."

"But we're in training!" Anna insisted in a hiss.

"Actually, there's nothing in the manual that says trainees cannot deliver the post." If I wasn't mistaken—and I definitely wasn't—it was actually encouraged for trainees to take on deliveries so they could learn the ropes through experience. Though it didn't mention dragon riders specifically. When both Andrés and Anna stared at me, though, I studied my shoes. "I, ah, memorised the manual. For the exam?"

The courier entrance exam, perhaps, but they didn't need to know that.

"The whole manual?" Andrés asked. I nodded.

"Are you going to load these crates or what?" Bartwell was no longer cowering at the mere sight of Zapyros, instead waving his hands uselessly while his son warily stacked crates next to my dragon. I went to help, loading them in the compartments on Zapyros's saddle, making sure the weight was evenly distributed at his direction. My belly churned with excitement. This was my first missive. My first assignment. And it wasn't even to anyone in Ilisar, but all the way in Dun Kennis to the south!

The crates loaded, I signed my name to the bottom of Bartwell's missive as proof of receipt, took the first page for my own records, and all but leaped onto Zapyros's back. He stretched and shook, beating his wings once to make sure everything was sitting properly.

"Well?" Zapyros asked archly at Pennytyne and Cyneric, both of whom were standing back, watching. "Are we going to fly or what?"

"But—"

"Yes!" Cyneric interrupted his rider, spreading his wings and showing his teeth. A dragon smile.

"Andrés?" Pennytyne nosed him, but it was

impossible to mistake the excitement in her own eyes. He looked around, as if half-expecting Markham and Clover to appear and tell us off. But Bartwell was already walking away, his beleaguered son dragging the empty cart behind him.

Zapyros lowered his head to Andrés, his amber eyes intense. "The more experience we have, the faster they'll release us to regular duties instead of this ridiculous training."

There was an undercurrent between the two that I didn't understand, something that had Andrés shifting his weight under Zapyros's stare. If I were to guess, I would have thought that my dragon was judging Andrés, sizing him up for something. But I was a poor judge of the unsaid, so I just sat in the saddle. Waiting.

"Very well," Andrés said, sighing. "I guess we do need the flying practise."

"Good! Then let's be off." In a snap of his wings, Zapyros leaped into the air, the loaded saddle not slowing him down in the slightest. Cyneric and Pennytyne followed after, wheeling through the air and earning shouts from their riders.

"You know the way to Dun Kennis?" I asked, already forming an image of the map in my mind.

"I have travelled beyond the walls of Ilisar

before, Little Bird," Zapyros grumbled. But he didn't protest when I pressed that map-image against the wall in my mind so he could see it, too. He tilted his wings, turned us south along the river, and then we were off. Couriers in truth for the first time.

CHAPTER 13

The flight to Dun Kennis was, according to the map, fairly straightforward. It was a smaller city along the river Brighly directly south of Ilisar. Even without my intimate knowledge of the map, we would be hard pressed to get lost so long as we followed the river. This meant that Zapyros felt free to goad Cyneric and Pennytyne into more involved flight manoeuvres.

"Twist! No, you must remember that you have a rider on your back," Zapyros snapped, his teeth coming within inches of Pennytyne's tail. She squeaked and righted herself, Andrés barely clinging to the saddle despite being strapped in. He turned to me, wide-eyed. I bit back a chuckle. It was nice not to be the one under Zapyros's intense training regimen for once. "You cannot bend that way and expect your rider to remain in their seat. They have to have something to hold on to."

"But when I fly by myself—"

"You are *not* by yourself!" Zapyros shot a stream of sparks through the air, startling Pennytyne enough that she dropped below the wardancer's belly, screeching her surprise. Windcatcher dove after them, flipping her wings at Zapyros in a gesture that even I could tell was incredibly rude.

"It's alright, Pen," Andrés said once the pair had rejoined the formation. He was breathing a bit hard and his hands were shaking when he patted his dragon's neck. "We'll try again."

"And you!" Zapyros turned his massive head to Cyneric, who was watching all of the scolding with a smug expression. He had mastered the twisting spiral fairly quickly. "Practise your diving!"

Cyneric snorted but dutifully folded his wings so that he fell into a gentle swoop towards the ground. Anna whooped and threw her arms in the air.

Zapyros growled. "A proper dive!" He opened his jaws and a stream of flame jetted out, just shy of Cyneric's tail. The red dragon roared and dove, heading towards the ground so quickly that Anna let out a cry of alarm. She leaned in, grabbing hold of the red fur down Cyneric's back and when he opened his wings, she was ready.

"Very good," Zapyros rumbled in approval. He tilted his head towards Pennytyne, who was now executing the twist with the proper tilt of her body. "Improvements, both of you."

"How far is Dun Kennis?" Anna asked, a slight wobble to her voice to match the green tinge in her cheeks. I considered our position over the river.

"We should be there by morning. Shortly after dawn, I would guess," I said, slightly surprised at the answer. We'd made better time than even I anticipated. Maybe there was something to this travel by dragonback. Zapyros was swift, even when slowing down to allow for the manoeuvres of the smaller courier dragons. And when they flew at their full speed, they were even faster than Zapyros, though he was better suited for distance flying.

"Morning!" Anna looked shocked. "Someone will notice we're gone. Can't we get there sooner?"

"The world is not small," Zapyros snapped. "Or did you think that couriers used dragons for long distances just for fun?"

"I never said—" Anna started, then stopped. "What is that?"

A small bird-like creature was flying towards us,

winging lazily through the air. As it drew closer, I saw that it was not a bird at all, though it had feathered wings and a feathered crest on its head. It was a dragon. A dragon with a razor sharp beak, four sets of needle-like talons, and a penchant for violence.

"Flutterling," I breathed, my alarm washing up against that wall in my mind enough that Zapyros snorted out sparks.

"Flutterling?" Andrés peered at the dragon, about half the size of Windcatcher, as it drew nearer. His voice, too, was quiet. "But don't they travel in flocks?"

The flutterling swooped around us then all but hovered in mid-air. Its tiny pink tongue darted out and an eager gleam crossed its eye. It opened its beak.

"Zapyros! Stop it!" I cried. Too late.

The flutterling screeched, the sound piercing, loud enough to echo across both sides of the river. Ahead of us, a cloud of colour burst forth from a stand of trees. The flutterling's flock. And they were coming right for us.

Zapyros roared belatedly and snapped his jaws at the tiny dragon. It wheeled back in a swift movement, diving to join its flock. They drew closer, the sound of hundreds of wings humming through the air. My stomach dropped.

"Get ready to fly, and fly fast," Zapyros said. I could hear a rumbling in his chest as he gathered his flames. The young courier dragons hesitated just behind him, unsure.

"Go!" I screamed, waving them on. "Go now!"

Pennytyne listened, flying off faster than I'd ever seen her move. Andres was tucked in close to her neck. She sliced through the air like an arrow, winging her way above the flutterling flock. For an instant, it looked like she would make it, that they would take no interest in her. Then, a handful of them broke off from the main flock and turned towards Pennytyne. By then, the main flock had reached us and I lost track of everything except saving my own hide.

Zapyros burned several of the flutterlings on his first breath of fire, but they were fast and manoeuvrable and they attacked with murderous intent. They went for the head, the eyes, their beaks digging in to the soft hide between Zapyros's scales, their talons piercing where their beaks couldn't reach. They flew towards me, too, snapping and biting and clawing, doing their best to tear the flesh from my bones.

Flutterlings were a menace, and I'd seen the results of their attacks before, but never had dealt with them myself. They liked to attack chicken and pigs primarily, and only very, very rarely went after cows, so my family's dairy farm had always been reasonably safe. Grimble had killed any stray flutterlings that ventured near our lands, not ever hesitating. He'd said that if you didn't kill the scouts, then the whole flock would appear, and you hardly stood a chance.

They were carnivorous, voracious, and completely without a sense of self-preservation. A perfect predator, if that predator were the size of a large songbird and travelled in flocks of hundreds.

Now, I understood Grimble's lack of hesitation. The flutterlings dove for me, claws outstretched. I cursed, loudly, and pulled my flight leather jacket over my head. I felt the tips of needles scrape my skin, the sensation like fire. Zapyros roared, shaking his body violently to dispel the flutterlings.

"Hold on, Little Bird. The air is going to get thin." The words came through our bond, a volley over the wall. Then, before I could ask, Zapyros surged forwards with heavy beats of his wings. He flew nearly vertical, ignoring the continued biting and clawing of the flutterlings. I pulled my head from

my leathers and found we were climbing for the clouds.

The air did get thin, and cold, but it was hardly noticeable when compared to the relief of the flutterlings falling away, not able to fly so high. Zapyros levelled off, shaking his head. I tried to ignore my own pain, looking instead for the others.

Pennytyne was a seafoam green speck in the distance, having managed to outfly the flutterlings with sheer speed. Cyneric, though, was still overset. He was twisting in midair, biting and snapping at the monsters. Anna was beating at them with her hands, trying to shield herself from the impossibly sharp beaks.

"Zapyros," I said.

"I see them."

"What do we do?" Nothing in the courier manual had said anything about having to defend yourself when on a job. Couriers were neutral. No one could touch them politically and they were never to be used as hostages or fodder in wars for fear of losing all mail privileges altogether. Most beasts would leave a dragon alone and those that didn't were usually few and far between, lingering at the edges of known territories. But flutterlings?

There was that rumbling in Zapyros's chest

again, louder than before. *"Hold on, Little Bird."* He folded his wings completely flat against his sides and we fell from the sky straight towards the desperate Cyneric and Anna.

The wind screamed in my ears. Had I not been wearing goggles, my eyes would be watering. I was grateful for the straps on the saddle that held me in place, because I knew that I would have been lost to the wind otherwise.

Zapyros dove, a creature of grace and deadly precision, holding his breath as he aimed for the writhing red courier dragon. He opened his mouth when we were a hundred feet above. A moment later, fire bloomed forth, a living thing reaching for the others.

Anna screamed.

Cyneric roared.

The flutterlings abandoned their prey at the sight of the fire reaching for them. They darted off in a swarm, heading for the same stand of trees from which they'd emerged. A moment later, I realised that was exactly what Zapyros had wanted them to do.

He snapped his wings open, angling them so we flew directly for the trees. Fire still streamed from between his teeth, bright and sulfuric and deadly.

The fleeing flutterlings didn't make it to their trees before they were consumed, the wardancer's fire hot enough to turn them to ash.

It had happened in an instant. A deadly instant, one which I'd never have been able to conceive of on my own. Zapyros cut off his fire and roared his success, scaring actual birds into flight, though no more flutterlings took to the skies. Had we been on the ground, the earth would have shaken. Instead, I felt the air tremble around us.

I understood in that moment just how deadly a dragon Zapyros was. Why everyone in the courier service was afraid and uncertain around him. He was no transport dragon. He was a harbinger of death.

"Can you still fly?" Zapyros called to Cyneric. I looked over my shoulder and saw the red dragon listing dangerously to one side. His wings looked like they'd been caught in flutterling claws.

"Yes," Cyneric snapped, tail twitching. He beat his wings and listed even further off centre.

"There is a field up ahead. Land there. I'll go bring Pennytyne back." Without consulting me, Zapyros beat his wings hard and fast, gaining on the green courier dragon. She circled warily some distance ahead, obviously wanting to fly onwards. Andrés, I saw, was waving his arms at us.

"The flutterlings are gone," Zapyros announced. "Cyneric is hurt. Come."

We all landed a few minutes later in the field; thankfully, it looked like it was being used for nothing more important than hay or grazing live-stock. It would be fine for having three dragons rest there a while. I unstrapped myself, frowning at the sight of blood on my hands. The flutterlings had scratched them quite badly, as well as my neck where I hadn't pulled the leathers up. My jacket was all but shredded, though the scratches on my arms and back were superficial because of its protection. Zapyros had a few cuts on his face, but none of them looked deep. Only one was still bleeding, and that slowly.

Anna, though, was badly hurt. Andrés was already helping her out of her saddle. Her leathers were badly torn. The flutterlings had taken a large chunk out of her right ear, cut her across the bridge of her nose, and scratched her chest and hands severely.

My heart was still racing, the noise of the battle still ringing in my ears.

"You are injured," Zapyros said, nudging me with his snout.

"I'll be fine." My voice sounded funny. I stumbled away from my dragon and went to Anna. Cyneric hissed, flaring his wings as he tried to wrap them around her. They were, indeed, full of holes.

"Don't be ridiculous, Cyneric," Anna said, her voice steadier than mine, though her hands trembled. "They're only trying to help."

"I have an aid pack in my kit. Kayleigh, will you get it for me? Front pouch on the left side." Andrés sounded the most reasonable of us all, his attention fully focused on Anna as though he did this sort of thing every day. I was more than a little grateful that one of us was relatively calm.

I went to Pennytyne and grabbed the pack. She hadn't been injured by the flutterlings, but she still snaked her head back and forth, agitated.

"We should never have gone out without permission," she mewled, digging her claws into the earth.

"Don't be foolish," Zapyros snarled, showing that his fangs were still tinged with char. "Flutterlings would have attacked anyone. And we survived, didn't we? You will face much worse in this world and you need to be prepared for it."

"We're not going to war," I said in an undertone. "We're couriers. Not soldiers."

Zapyros reared back as if struck. His blade-tipped tail sliced through the grasses of the field and his wings flared. He bared his teeth. Then, in an instant, he relaxed and sank to the ground, laying his head flat so I could look directly into one great eye.

"Perhaps you are right," he said, and those words were full of a pain that I was certain I would never understand.

CHAPTER 14

Despite the fact that I'd learned from a young age how to tend injuries—my mother was exasperated with my constant clumsiness, so taught me to deal with my own scrapes and bruises instead—I was relegated to sitting by the wayside while Andrés tended Anna's wounds. Apparently, my bedside manner was abrasive. Or so Zapyros said. No one else disagreed.

Cyneric was more concerned with his rider's hurts than his own, though his wings looked to be in rough shape. He'd snapped at Pennytyne when she nosed them, folding them close to his body. That was all he'd allowed until we saw to Anna.

"Thankfully, most of these are superficial," Andrés said, cleaning the last of the scratches on her face. "Though I'm afraid there's nothing I can do about your ear."

"Is it bad?" Anna lifted a hand to the injured ear, stopping short of actually touching it since Andrés had applied a poultice and bandage already.

"No one will notice," Andrés said.

"You're missing a piece about this big," I said, holding up the first knuckle of my finger. "Only it's in a wedge shape. Like the flutterling just bit it out."

Andrés shot me a wide-eyed look.

"I mean, I guess people won't notice if you keep your hair over your ear." I tried for a friendly smile, but Andrés's expression only grew more alarmed, so I gave up. Anna snorted a laugh.

"You really don't pull your punches, huh, Kayleigh? Maybe I'll be lucky enough to find a healer with actual magic who can piece it together. Other-wise I'll just have to pierce it and wear something sparkly. A chain, perhaps?" Anna's hand fluttered up to her ear again before pulling away. She gently shoved Andrés back. "Go away. I'm fine. I need to tend to Cyneric, anyways."

The red dragon lifted his head as she approached, hissing a bit before relenting and spreading his wings for his rider to examine. I

watched curiously, my thoughts dull. Shock, probably. Sensory overload, definitely.

Andrés sat before me. "Your turn."

I flinched back as he took my wrist to look at my
hand.

"Sorry! Did I hurt you?" His voice was quieter, a
murmur instead of loud and I was relieved for the
reprieve from the noise.

"No. It's just..." I hunched my shoulders.

"Little Bird?" Zapyros moved closer, his talons
digging furrows in the earth. "What is it?"

"I just...I don't usually like people touching me."
When that earned me a horrified look from Andrés
and a growl from Zapyros, I hastened to clarify. "It's
nothing bad! It's just that people all do it wrong.
Touch me, I mean. Well, not wrong, per se, it's just
uncomfortable most of the time but not if they do it
right and—"

"Kayleigh." A smile twitched at the corner of
Andrés's mouth. "It's alright. Why don't you tell me
how to touch you correctly?"

My cheeks heated. That sounded, even to my
ears, decidedly like innuendo and if there was
anything that I wasn't good at, it was innuendo. I
quickly averted my eyes to my hands. "Er. Well.
Um." I took a breath. "Okay. I like it when the touch

is heavy. Solid. Not a brush across my skin or half-hearted hand holding. It has to be firm. Like a weighted blanket or a tight hug. Everything else feels like ants crawling over my skin and I hate it."

"Like this?" Andrés took my wrist again, this time his touch as solid as the ground beneath my feet. It wasn't perfunctory, like some people I'd known well enough to tell my preferences, but heavy. Firm. Friendly. And the spark that travelled from his fingers to mine was something I'd never felt before. I liked it.

"Exactly like that." I watched, fascinated, as he cleaned the scratches on my hand with a swift but firm hand. He was skilled beyond my own mild capabilities, like he'd done this before many times. I watched as he moved on to my other hand, then found myself meeting his eyes when he lifted my chin to tend to a cut on my neck.

Time moved slowly for a heartbeat. Long enough that I could see gold flecked in his eyes between blinks. I looked away first, as usual, shifting my gaze to a point just over his shoulder. "Where did you learn to do this?"

"My father's guards taught me." Andrés dabbed at the deepest cut hard enough for me to be comfortable, though it did hurt, what with the wound. I bit back a hiss. "I was forever following them around. Training. Pretending I could do what they did. Eventually, they decided that I might as well learn *something*, since it was fairly clear that I would never be much good with weapons."

He smirked, catching my gaze again. "As evidenced by my attempts at the festival."

"You are exceptionally bad at games," I agreed. Andrés rubbed a bit of poultice over the last of my scratches and pulled back.

"There. Better?"

"Thank you." I wasn't quite sure where to put my hands, to look. Andrés was still sitting there, smiling at me. He wasn't touching me anymore, but I could have sworn that I still felt the phantom sparks that his touch had caused. "Um. Well, Zapyros and I had better get going if we want to deliver the post in a timely fashion."

This statement drew the attention of everyone in the field. Anna, cupping Cyneric's jaw in her hands while she examined him, whipped around to stare at me. "You can't be serious."

"Well, not *you*. Obviously, you have to go back to Ilisar. And you, too, Andrés, Pennytyne. You should go with them in case they need help on the way. But Zapyros and I have accepted this missive, so we have to deliver the post." It was a rule. A courier could, theoretically, turn back and discharge their post to another courier, but only under the most dire of circumstances. Being attacked by flutterlings was unfortunate, but it was hardly worth turning around for. Besides, we were the only transport-class dragon and rider pair this side of the continent. Zapyros could still fly, the crates were still intact, and we were already well on the way to Dun Kennis.

"You can't go alone!" Andrés protested. I frowned.

"She won't be alone," Zapyros said, finally lifting his head and stretching his jaws in a yawn. "She has me. Go back to Ilisar. Report the flutterling attack, get your wounds seen to. We shall be there and back again within a day and a half."

None of the others seemed to want to argue with Zapyros like they wanted to argue with me. Perhaps it was the fact that he had flame-broiled a swarm of vicious, if tiny, dragons. Or perhaps it was that he was already extending a leg for me to climb up to his back. Or maybe they just trusted him more. Whatever the reason, it rankled a bit.

"Hey, Kayleigh. Be careful, alright?" Andrés waited until I looked him in the eye and gave a firm nod before he relaxed his shoulders. He nodded in return and went to Pennytyne. Windcatcher, perched on her back, immediately launched herself to his shoulder, nuzzling him fiercely.

"You know Markham is going to be furious that you went on by yourself," Anna murmured. For once it was she who wouldn't look at me. "If it was all three of us, then maybe he'd be okay. But just you? He'll report you."

It wasn't fair. Surely he had to give up on his ridiculous persecution eventually. I was just doing my job! I said nothing, just nodded. Anna backed towards Cyneric. "Be careful."

Zapyros let out a roar, beating his wings once before he leaped into the air and angled us back down the river. "Careful. Ha! They know not with whom you ride."

I patted his neck, though I doubted he could feel me through his thick hide. Then, I settled in for a long ride, lost in my thoughts.

CHAPTER 15

We made it to Dun Kennis about an hour after dawn. Zapyros had flown through the night without complaint. The one time I'd suggested we rest until morning, he'd snorted out a handful of sparks and refused to reply. I think my suggestion only made him fly faster.

I slept as best I could, but I was still groggy and bleary-eyed when we landed. The saddle had ample room to lay down, but it was far from comfortable for sleeping. Not to mention the constant wind from flying was maddening. I would have to pack earplugs next trip. Or ear muffs. Something. Anything to keep my sanity intact.

We landed in a field just on the edge of town and

Zapyros and I walked the rest of the way. I did my best to stifle my yawns in front of other people. I was representing the Guild, after all.

Zapyros had no such compunctions. At least two farmers hurried away in alarm at the sight of his fangs.

Dun Kennis was a town blessed with rich soil and close proximity to the river. It produced a goodly portion of the food for the surrounding regions and was known for its disproportionate number of cooks. And taverns.

We stopped at the first tavern we saw, a place just opening for those workers looking for an early breakfast. I asked for Hadrian Nadreth and was directed to a farm on the other end of town. It was a large place, well kept and with at least twenty people working there, moving hay or tilling the fields, plucking weeds, harvesting the first of the summer fruits.

"Hadrian Nadreth?" I asked one of the workers. They jerked their thumb over their shoulder towards a dark-skinned man with a truly impressive beard and a pot belly. He leaned over a scythe with a sharpening stone.

"Hadrian Nadreth?" I asked.

"Yep. What do you—oh. Oh." He had seen Zapyros. His eyes went wide, and he nearly dropped the sharpening stone.

"My name is Kayleigh Espinosa, rider of Zapyros, representing the Courier's Guild. I have a special delivery for you from Bartwell and Sons. Ten crates." I pulled out the missive and handed over the farmer's receipt. He took it, still staring at Zapyros.

"That's a wardancer," he breathed, leaning close to me.

"Yes. I know. I rode him here. Do you take receipt of the crates?"

"What's a wardancer doing in the courier service?"

"A transport dragon recently retired, and he was transferred from the Aerial Corp. Do you take receipt of the crates?" Something in my tone must have snapped him out of himself. He nodded fervently, still looking severely alarmed.

"Yes. I do. Now please hurry and unload those crates before I have the whole town coming to ask why a wardancer is in my farmyard." Hadrian quickly signed his name with the pen I provided and shoved the paper back at me. Zapyros was already lowering himself to the ground so I could unload the crates. If I had hoped for help from the workers, I was not going to get it. I took each crate from the saddle and set it a distance away. Only then would the workers take it. Zapyros rolled his eyes at the theatrics and said nothing. I, on the other hand, was fuming.

Within an hour, we were heading away from the farm and back to the tavern where we'd first stopped. By silent agreement, neither of us mentioned the ridiculous treatment Zapyros had received, instead going straight for breakfast. I purchased a warm roll with cheese for me and a side of beef for Zapyros. He ate the whole thing in two bites, earning stares from not only the people, but the dragon guarding the tavern, a small copper creature who looked more inclined towards laying before the fire than guarding precious resources.

"You're rather large," the little dragon said. He was barely as tall as my hip at the top of his head.

"And you're not," Zapyros commented just as rudely.

"Perhaps I would be that big if they fed me a side of beef?" The dragon looked hopefully at the woman who emerged from the kitchen door with a bucket of meat for the spits.

"Not going to happen," she said simply. To me, she said, "I hate to rush you, Courier, but your dragon is making the customers a might uncomfortable. Something about how sharp his claws are. For my part, you can stay as long as you like, but the owner is starting to get frustrated."

Zapyros showed his fangs. "My teeth are equally sharp, Mistress."

The woman nodded, expression flat. Her mouth twitched like she was holding back a smile. "I can see that. Courier?"

Even I could see what she wanted, though she was at least apologetic about it. My tone was crisp when I said, "My thanks for the food. And for trying to let me stay. Zapyros, can you fly?"

"I can fly two days without sleep or food," Zapyros said primly, extending his leg for me to climb. "This was hardly a challenge."

I snorted, settling into my saddle. Zapyros had the decency to walk to the field before spreading his wings and leaping into the air, leaving Dun Kennis behind.

Finally, I couldn't take it any longer. "How dare they—"

"Hush, Kayleigh," Zapyros said, sighing.

"But the way they treated you!"

"Is no more than I have received many times over. Just as you have. We neither of us can help being what we are, and while it is annoying to have to put up with other people's stumbling and staring and ill-thought words, does that change anything for us? About us?"

I huffed. "No. We are the same as before."

"Do you expect me to burn down the house of everyone who thinks you odd?"

"That would be ridiculous," I muttered. "People are just...I see your point."

Zapyros turned his head to look at me. He looked smug. I scowled.

"If it matters, *I* don't think you're going to suddenly go on a violent rampage." I sniffed and rubbed the scales in front of me, as though my touch could provide some sort of comfort. Zapyros chuckled, the sound rumbling through the saddle and vibrating my bones.

"It matters quite a bit. Thank you."

We flew on up the river, which was coming alive with the day's activities. Boats move smoothly on the water, steered by fisher folk looking to catch their next meal. Birds swooped down to eat insects rising off the water. Thankfully, there were no signs of flutterlings. It looked to be a lovely day.

"Well, Little Bird? How does it feel to have completed your first courier assignment?" Zapyros asked after we'd been flying for nearly an hour.

I frowned, tracing the letters carved into the saddle in front of me. Had we really just done that? We had. I'd just completed a delivery start to finish and now no one could say that I wasn't a courier. That I wasn't fit. I thought of my family and couldn't help but wonder what they would say. Papi would be thrilled. Mami would huff and change the subject, then pretend she had never doubted. Carmen would say nothing at all, just run after her husband and children and demand I help.

But I'd done it. At least to myself, I'd proven the world wrong. I held that little spark close. "It feels wonderful."

"Is it everything you wanted? You...you don't regret becoming a rider?" There was a hint of vulnerability in Zapyros's voice.

"It's everything I wanted and more." I considered. "Though, next time I might bring my supplies and draw a map on the way. I never thought about what to do while flying long distances."

Zapyros barked out a laugh, sparks flying through the air. "You are certainly unique, Kayleigh Espinosa. Not at all what I expected."

"And what exactly did you expect?" I demanded.

Zapyros laughed again. "I expected to be bored. And you are anything but boring. Now, let's get back. Surely Markham is foaming at the mouth to enact some punishment for us."

My good mood deflated. I settled into the saddle with a sigh and tried not to imagine the consequences for this little excursion. As we flew, though, I held tightly to the fact that I was a courier in truth, now. And no one, not even Markham and Clover, could take that from me.

CHAPTER 16

I hesitated in the infirmary doorway, shifting my weight and wondering wether I should just return later. Or not at all. I was tired after the long journey and maybe Anna wouldn't want to see me. Maybe it would be better just to—

"Kayleigh!" Anna waved me in. She was sitting on a bench, a young healer assigned to the Courier Guild prodding at one of the deeper cuts with a cotton cloth. "Ow! Come on in. Save me from this mutilation."

The healer snorted, shaking her head. "It's not my fault that they can do nothing for the ear. I have no magic, and even if I did, the damage is done. Even magic cannot regrow...that."

Anna huffed then turned her attention to me. "You made it back okay? No problems?"

I shook my head. "Package delivered. No sign of flutterlings on the flight home. And I just turned in the paperwork to the clerks so everything is sorted on this end."

My answer did not appear to satisfy Anna. She narrowed her eyes at me. "No issues with Markham? No...confrontations?"

"He was not even here when Zapyros and I arrived. Neither he nor Clover. Why? Did he give *you* problems?"

Anna shook her head. The healer bit back a laugh that was more bite than mirth. "He was in here shouting at you not an hour gone, and don't you deny it. You riders think you're so tough, but I'll not have that sort of disruptive behaviour in my infirmary. It's bad for the healing process."

"He was a bit upset." Anna glared at the healer. "But Andrés already submitted a report to Master Templeton—"

"Why would he do that?" There was no reason for one of the leaders of the Guild to get involved. It was a simple delivery, excepting the situation with the flutterlings, and I doubted that they were cause for Templeton's involvement.

"Because Markham has been cruel and abusive to you?" Anna said this as though it were obvious. I frowned. She meant Andrés had made a report about Markham, not the delivery to Dun Kennis. Somehow, that was worse. "We knew that you would probably be removed from the service if Markham got wind of what you'd done before you had a chance to argue your side. So we got there first. And I made sure that Andrés included *everything* in his report."

My frown became a scowl. "The situation was well in hand."

"The situation had the man supposed to be training you calling you out for no reason in front of everyone else. Loudly. I don't even think Andrés was the first to submit a report."

We hadn't been that loud, had we? I winced. Quieter, I repeated, "The situation was well in hand."

Anna reached out and took my hand, squeezing tightly. She must have been listening when I explained my preferences to Andrés. I blinked, astonished. "You don't have to do everything on your own, you know," she murmured. "It's okay to have help."

I shrugged my shoulders up to my ears and said

nothing, shifting my weight. In my experience that was not always, or even often, the case. I'd been made to feel a burden every time I asked for help in my family, except from my papi, and even he was too busy for me to want to disturb him often. In my mami's eyes, anytime I needed help was proof that I would never be more than her Changeling child, difficult and odd.

Anna squeezed my hand again. Before I fled the room, I blurted out, "Thanks." Then, awkward conversation over, I turned on my heel and all but ran out.

In a corner of my mind near that wall, I heard the laugh of Zapyros echoing.

It was two days before anything of interest happened regarding Andrés's report. I slept for a good portion of those two days, emerging for meals and checking to see if there were any orders for me before returning to my rooms to read or draw my maps of our journey. Training, it would seem, had been cancelled while Markham was away. Whatever that meant.

Zapyros, surprisingly, did not insist that we

continue our after-hours training sessions during that time, claiming that he was tired from the journey and wanted to sleep. My guess was that he was just tired of my company as we had been together constantly for the last three days and, even soulbonded, that much interaction was grating. Then again, I would occasionally get feelings of deep, contented sleep from over the wall in my mind.

The morning of the third day dawned with a sky full of clouds and a rainstorm that pounded relentlessly on the walls of the Guild building. I was struggling to stay awake during the morning meal, pouring heaping spoonfuls of sugar in my tea, when Anna and Andrés and Nalia's rider, Ferran sat down, practically surrounding me.

"Did you hear?" Anna asked with barely contained glee. Her scratches were all but healed, except for the hole in her ear, which she had indeed adorned with decorative rings and a chain, as she promised to do.

"That we're meant to be flying manoeuvres in this weather?" I glared at the high windows in the dining hall. They were splattered with water. "I know that the Guild promises delivery no matter the weather, but surely—"

"No, not the rain!" Anna rolled her eyes. "Markham!"

Dread settled in my belly. I stabbed a sausage with my fork and frowned at the meat. I didn't even like sausage. Why was it on my plate?

Andrés tapped the table in front of me twice; I lifted my gaze from the sausage and found myself caught in his bright gaze. He was looking at me with intensity, the sort that turned the dread in my stomach to an entirely different sort of butterfly. I looked away, the eye contact too intense.

"He's gone, Kayleigh," Andrés said softly.

"What?" I dropped my fork to my plate, sausage and all. "What do you mean, gone?"

"Templeton had him reassigned to the Guild in Menaris on account of his actions here." Andrés grinned at me.

"Menaris, but that's—"

"On the other side of the Greenvale," Ferran said with a nod. He, too, looked pleased with this news. "He won't ever bother us again."

I sat back in my chair, not quite sure how to react. A great part of me was relieved—more than relieved—that I wouldn't have to deal with Markham again. I'd dealt with people who didn't understand me my whole life, but that was normal for a Fey Spirited. The palpable dislike that he'd displayed, though? That was different. And I was self-aware enough to acknowledge my relief.

But I was also disconcerted. I liked handling my own problems. To have not only Anna and Andrés involved, but Master Templeton, and to the point where they'd exiled—transferred—Markham, well that was hard for me.

"You don't look pleased," Andrés said.

"I'm not *dis*pleased," I replied carefully.

Anna snorted and folded her arms. "Let me guess. You had the situation well in hand? Take the win, Kayleigh. Be glad he's gone and that you'll never have to deal with him again. That *we'll* never have to deal with him again."

I smiled a bit. Just a bit. "Yeah. I guess that is really nice."

"Good! Because when you hear the rest of our news, you'll be in a really good mood." Anna waved at Ferran, who leaned forwards as if sharing a great secret.

"They're going to hold The Great Race this year. And we're qualified to participate!"

CHAPTER 17

I ran into my mother just as I was coming out of the flight supplies store. I'd ordered a new set of leather ear muffs to block out the wind, since the wax plugs that were standard issue for couriers didn't block out enough for me. Zapyros insisted that every bit of gear I owned be perfect in both comfort and function before the Great Race. He was taking it even more seriously than the other courier dragons, despite the fact that there was only one other dragon in the transport class against whom we were competing. In fact, he was becoming a bit insufferable about it.

"Kayleigh!"

I stumbled, nearly dropping my muffs. "Mami?" Dread coiled in my belly. I hadn't seen her since that day all those months ago when I'd first bonded with Zapyros.

She looked the same as ever, dressed elegantly with her hair done in braids and pinned up like a crown. She had a basket over her arm and my sister Carmen was just behind her, also carrying some shopping. Market day. The only day that she would bother coming into the city.

"Kayleigh!" Mami thrust the basket back at Carmen and before I knew what was happening, had wrapped her arms around me, squeezing tightly, just the way I liked. "I'm so glad to see you!"

I patted her back awkwardly. "Hello, Mami."

She pulled away and held my shoulders, looking me over. "How are you? Are you enjoying your job? Your Papi says that you passed your training without any difficulties, as if there would be. Have you been eating enough? I know how you forget sometimes when you're hyperfocused on something. Are you competing in the Great Race? It's all any of the dragons can talk about, even Grimble. Apparently it only happens once a decade. Of course, you will do spectacularly."

I blinked, a little stunned. She was acting like everything was normal, like the fight between us—those horrible words—had never happened. Maybe that was good? Skip right over the awkwardness and get on with having a normal-ish relationship. No. Something in my stomach twisted at that. I smiled as best I could before answering her questions. "I'm good. I love being a courier, especially with Zapyros. I passed my training. I've been eating; meals are included in my room and board. We are going to compete in the Great Race. Zapyros seems to think he can beat even the courier dragons handily, though we're technically in the transport class."

Mami nodded, but she didn't look happy at my words. She tightened her grip on my shoulders and clicked her tongue. "You have...lines around your eyes. Too much sun."

I touched my face self-consciously. "They're from the flight goggles. I was out delivering packages the last few days and only got back this morning. They'll go away."

"I think the look suits you," Carmen said, smirking.

"Ay, Carmen! Don't be rude to your sister. This is what she wants." Mami waved a hand vaguely in my direction, focusing on my face. I wasn't terribly surprised by this turn of the conversation, but I was disappointed. I wondered what sort of excuse would get me away and back to the Guild Hall. I could pretend to be sick. Or maybe I had flight practise this afternoon? Yes, that would work. I opened my mouth and was immediately cut off.

"I know I said horrible things to you, Kayleigh," Mami started, stunning me even more. She wasn't one to apologise. Ever. But now, she looked genuinely regretful, her gaze a bit sad. "I was wrong to say them, to even think them. You can do anything you set your mind to, and I was wrong to doubt you. I just...I worry. Do you forgive me?"

I nodded, certain my eyes were as wide as dinner plates. "Of course I forgive you, Mami." Yes, the things she'd said cut me to the bone, but I believed she regretted them. I'd proven to both her and myself that I could do this, without a doubt. And now? With her standing before me, apologising, how could I do anything but forgive her?

She sniffled once before straightening and beaming at me. "There is a party tonight for your Gran's birthday. You will come, yes? I am making strawberry cake, her favourite." Mami gestured to the basket Carmen was holding, full of strawberries. "She would like to see you. Your Papi, too. Marco will be back from selling the cattle, so everyone will be home. You will come, yes, or do I have to disappoint your Gran?"

Ah, the guilt trip. I was intimately familiar with this tactic, and just as susceptible as I had been as a girl. I winced. "I, ah, had plans with a friend—"

"Bring them! We always make enough food to feed several dragons, not to mention one courier." Mami nodded firmly, and I knew there would be no arguments. Carmen rolled her eyes behind my mother's back. Before I could say anything further, Mami took her basket from my sister and strode off to go finish the shopping.

I slumped against the wall of the flight shop, suddenly exhausted.

"Was that your family?"

I jumped and cursed. Andrés stood on the corner, laughing. "You *and* Zapyros need bells. Seriously! You're sneaks, the both of you."

"I was just coming to drop off my jacket for repair." He held up his flight leathers and wiggled a finger through a hole in the shoulder seam. "No matter how many times the Guild people repair it, it never fits right. So I thought they might be able to do better here. I caught the last bit of your conversation. Your family?"

I nodded. "My mother and sister. I have been summoned home for my grandmother's birthday."

"Sounds fun. Then, I always like birthdays."

I narrowed my eyes at Andrés, considering. Before I could rethink this harebrained scheme, I blurted out, "Will you come with me? Only, I told my mother that I had plans with a friend but she said to bring them, and I thought maybe if you weren't busy—"

Andrés's smile widened. "Sure. I'd be happy to come, Kayleigh."

"Don't be so eager to agree. My family is…loud." I frowned. "Very loud. And they like to poke at each other. Verbally, I mean, though my sister's children can be quite physical when they get too much energy. And my mother—"

Andrés reached out and squeezed my hand. Tightly. Tension flowed out of me at the unexpected touch. My shoulders relaxed. "It's okay. I understand. My family can be difficult, too. If my being there will help you, then I'm happy to come."

I flushed and stared at my toes. "Oh. Thanks. Um, meet me outside the hall at seven? I'll see if Zapyros will fly us to the farm. Otherwise it's a three mile walk."

"I'll see you at seven. Do I need to bring anything?"

I shook my head. "I don't think so. It's just dinner with my family. They'll make all the food."

"I'll bring flowers, then. Just in case."

Before I could react to that, he entered the shop, throwing a grin over his shoulder just as the door closed behind him. I frowned at the door. There were some things I just wasn't going to understand about people. Instead of trying to puzzle that particular look out—or worse, go into the shop and *ask* him—I turned on my heel and started back to the Guild hall.

What a day this was turning out to be. I could just imagine the look Zapyros would give me when he discovered our evening plans. He hadn't asked about meeting my family, but I had no doubt that he would be thrilled. The dragon loved to meddle.

I sighed and walked a little slower back to the hall. Zapyros was sleeping in the field while the rest of the hall went about their business. We were entitled to a full day off after doing a transport run, though we'd rarely taken it. Maybe it would be good to—

"I can feel you thinking, Little Bird," Zapyros mumbled, turning his muzzle towards me. He cracked open on large eye and waited.

"Um, we've been invited to my family farm for my Gran's birthday. Seven. Could you...Andrés is coming, too, and, well—"

"Your family?" As expected, that piqued his interest. Both his eyes opened, and he studied me intently. He even went so far as to sniff me. "You do not talk much about your family."

I winced. "It's, ah, complicated. My mami and I don't really get on. I mean, I thought we did, and then I became your rider and then..." I waved my hand vaguely.

Zapyros lifted his head and looked, strangely, abashed. "Do you mean that I caused—"

"No!" I assured him quickly. "No, it's nothing like that. It was just that she thought I couldn't really do this, and was just waiting for me to fail at being a courier anyways, and expected me to come back and live at home and just help out, because of my being Fae Spirited and all. It's not your fault."

Much to my alarm, this only made Zapyros growl and dig his talons into the ground. "That anyone would doubt you is folly, but your own mother did so? Just wait until I get my claws on her."

I gaped at my dragon. "It's not like that! She loves me, and I love her." At his narrowed eyes, I added, "Truly. It's just that we don't really understand each other's lives and interests and ways of thinking."

And wasn't that really it? I did love her, and I

didn't doubt that she loved me, but skies above, she baffled me sometimes.

Zapyros watched me for a moment before settling his head back onto the earth, though not before nuzzling me. "I will reserve judgement, for your sake, Little Bird. But remember that you are *my* family. Now and always, no matter what."

A wave of affection surged over the wall in my mind. I smiled and scratched the ridge of his nose. "And you are mine. No matter what."

CHAPTER 18

Andrés did bring flowers. He also dressed up in a nice black silk tunic that hugged the muscles of his arms and had me flushing for no good reason whatsoever. I wore my favourite dress—blue, made of a lightweight fabric that felt like wearing a cloud—and tried hard not to fidget with the end of my braid.

"Where is Windcatcher?" I blurted before he could greet me properly.

"She's with Pennytyne. She ate too much at lunch and decided she didn't want to go out again, the little lump." Andrés laughed good-naturedly. I nodded and tried to laugh, too, but it felt strange to see him without the little dragon. A moment later and I decided that it was nice to have him to myself for a bit. A moment after that and I pushed such thoughts aside for the silliness they were.

Zapyros narrowed his eyes at Andrés as we approached, but thankfully said nothing on the quick flight to my family's farm.

"Don't scare the cattle," I reminded him as we landed. "Grimble will be upset."

"As if I would bother frightening cows or antagonising your family's sworn herding dragon," Zapyros scoffed. He folded his wings on his back and settled into a crouch in the front pasture, which had been cleared of cows this time of night. Grimble raced up, spines bristling, wings flared, teeth flashing.

"Who are you?!" he growled, flexing his claws. Compared to Zapyros, the herding dragon was tiny, no larger than a regular horse and with none of the graceful lines of the wardancer. Still, Zapyros lowered his head respectfully.

"I am the courier Zapyros. Kayleigh Espinosa is my rider."

I waved to Grimble. "Hello."

The herding dragon sniffed. "You're back, I see. And in the company of...others. You'd better go in before you're late." With that, Grimble flipped his wings at us and marched to the back pasture and his herd.

"Good to see you, too," I muttered.

Zapyros tossed his head. "Some dragons have no manners."

"As if you don't growl at anyone who gets too close to Kayleigh," Andrés said, laughing. "Lead the way, Kayleigh."

"I'll make sure someone comes and brings you something to eat," I said to Zapyros before turning to the house with great reluctance. It looked exactly the same as it had done when I left, at least from the outside. I wondered if anything had changed inside or if it would be just as I'd left it, as if no time had passed at all. As if I hadn't changed.

"Are you alright?" Andrés nudged me with his shoulder and I realised I'd been walking slower the closer we got.

"Fine," I said. "Or, I will be once this is over. Don't be surprised if you get interrogated. Or if my mother draws certain conclusions. Or says things that are rude. Or—"

"I'll be alright," Andrés assured me. "I know a thing or two about difficult families, remember?"

I knocked on the door. Then, when nobody answered, opened it. "Hello?" I called.

Two blurs ran past, squealing as they escaped into the night. They waved a greeting at me but didn't slow down. "My sister's children," I said, introducing Andrés to their retreating backs. "You won't see them again for the rest of the evening."

"Who left the door open?" Carmen asked, stalking towards us with a swish of her elaborate skirts. She paused when she spotted me. "Oh. It's you." Her eyes widened when she spotted Andrés, and suddenly she was all charm and smiles.

"Welcome! Kayleigh said she was bringing someone, but I thought, well, you know," Carmen said, waving a dismissive hand with a flourish of her wrist. "Come in! Come in! I'm Carmen, Kayleigh's sister."

"A pleasure to meet you," Andrés said with a bow. "I'm Andrés Mierza."

Something sharpened in Carmen's eyes and she looked at me as though I'd been caught hiding some great secret. "Really? Well, it's nice to know that Kayleigh has decent friends. Let me introduce you to everyone."

I was certain that I was missing something, but the moment passed as Carmen swept us inside and then slipped her arm through Andrés's as she introduced him to Marco, Mami, Papi, Granda, and finally Gran. Andrés bowed deeply before my grandmother, handing over the bouquet of flowers.

"Happy birthday," he said, kissing her hand. She blushed beet red and buried her nose in the flowers.

"So charming!" she whispered to Granda. He nodded absently, peering back towards the kitchen, where fragrant smells filled the air. Mami and Gran fussed over the flowers, praising Andrés, and I wandered over to Papi.

"Kayleigh." He pulled me into a quick hug and pulled away just as quickly. The perfect amount of contact. "I hear you've been making waves with the Guild. People are talking about how Ilisar finally has a transport dragon again after the last two retired."

I imagined they were talking more about the fact that the transport dragon was a wardancer and therefore likely dangerous, but I played along. "I've been busy, that's for sure. We've been out three times in the last week."

"Oh? Anywhere very far?"

I shook my head. "Mostly a day or two's worth of flying at the most. The other transport dragon is stationed in Zasia so they take care of the western side of Amontyr. We'll meet them properly for the Great Race."

"Kayleigh!" Carmen called my name, gesturing towards the kitchen. "Come help with the roast."

I shrugged at Papi, who smiled indulgently, and then went to help my sister. Mami and Carmen had likely spent all day cooking, I realised, except for that brief stop to the market. There was a roast in the brick oven, heavy enough to require two people to pull it out. There were piles of flatbread and dipping sauces, salsas and vegetable fillings. A whole pan of roasted eggplant with a sesame and onion sauce. Another basket of fresh rolls with freshly whipped homemade butter. Cheeses of varying sources, some I recognised as being from our farm, others from the goat farmers down the road and one from a creamery that was known for the fruit-infused soft cheeses that went so perfectly with sweet bread and honey. And, to top it all off, Gran's favourite strawberry cake with a shining glaze.

"Wow," I said, mouth watering. "This looks amazing."

"Thank you," Carmen said, flushing a little. "You know Mami. She likes doing parties properly."

I hummed in agreement. Parties were Mami's specialty. "Do you think she'd mind if I made a plate for Zapyros before we sat down?"

"Zapyros?" Mami bustled into the kitchen, already casting a critical eye over the arrayed dishes and sniffing at the roast. She nodded approval before turning back to me. "Who is Zapyros?"

"My dragon," I said with a sheepish smile. "He flew Andrés and me here and I promised I'd bring him some food."

For a moment, alarm flared bright and clear in Mami's eyes. Then, she gathered herself. "Do you mean to tell me that your dragon has been sitting alone in the yard while we've been in here?"

I shifted my weight. "Er, yes, but—"

"There will be no buts! Kayleigh, prepare a plate. Carmen, get Marco and have him set the warming fires on the patio. We're eating outside tonight. No guest of any kind will be left alone at my house!" Mami clapped her hands and waved us off, picking up the eggplant dish and bustling out of the kitchen to announce the change of plans to everyone.

I piled the plate high with food, knowing that it wouldn't be much more than a quick bite to Zapyros, but wanting to make sure that he wouldn't miss out. By the time I had everything, the entire family was outside on the patio, arranging tables and chairs and talking loudly. Zapyros watched all of this from the yard with interest. He moved closer when I appeared, plate in hand.

"Has something happened?" he asked in a low rumble, sounding more than a little suspicious.

"Er, well, Mami didn't want you to be alone while we ate. It's rude to leave a guest by themselves, I think, even though you won't fit in the house." I'd explained this to him before we left and he assured me he was fine with the arrangement. Twice.

Still, the sudden warmth that flowed over the wall in my mind was a surprise. I felt badly for thinking I could leave the massive dragon on his own, even for something so terrifying as a birthday party with my family. Zapyros didn't deserve to be left out.

"I made you a plate," I said, holding the dish up. Before Zapyros could take it, I felt people crowding at my back. My family—all of them, including the distant Granda—were staring up at my dragon, mouths agape.

"Kayleigh," Mami hissed, nudging me with her elbow. "Introductions!"

Zapyros chuckled, the sound making Mami flinch. I'd forgotten how much like a growl it was.

"Everyone, this is Zapyros, my dragon. Zapyros,

this is Carmen, my sister, her husband Marco, my Mami, Papi, Gran and Granda. Carmen and Marco's kids ran off earlier, but they might turn up at some point."

"The two small ones with brown hair?" Zapyros nodded his great head. Mami's eyes followed the spikes and spines and horns with wide-eyed astonishment. "Yes, we met. They ran off towards the woods, I believe, looking for...crickets? Grimble went after them."

Carmen groaned. "They'll be muddy messes by the time they get back."

"Lovely to meet you, Zapyros," my father said with a slight bow. "Kayleigh has told me a great deal about you."

It wasn't exactly true, given that my communication with him had been via letters, but it was close enough that I let it be. Zapyros bowed his head in return.

"An honour to meet the esteemed family of my soulbound rider." Zapyros sniffed the air, drawing close to the plate still in my hands. Carmen let out a little squeak as Zapyros's massive head came within biting distance. "Is that...an orange-glazed roast I smell?"

Mami's instincts as a good host kicked in, her

astonishment replaced instantly with preening. "Orange and ginger. With pepper, rosemary and a hint of cumin."

Zapyros's tongue darted out and picked the piece of roast off the place. He hummed in approval. "My compliments to the chef!"

With that simple phrase, my dragon won over my mother, and thus, my entire family.

CHAPTER 19

The rest of the evening progressed as parties at the Espinosa house are wont to do. We all sat around the table, everyone else talking and telling stories while I listened in contented silence, eating food until it was impossible to stuff in another bite, at which point Marco and Papi went off to fetch their guitars and the music box, the only magical item we owned. It played just about any song, so long as someone played or sang along with it, no matter how badly. Then, everyone either listened to the music or, on rare occasions, started dancing.

"Dance with me!" Marco grabbed Carmen's hand before she could start clearing away dishes, leaving Papi to play along with the music box. They spun around the patio, Carmen more than a little tipsy on wine and laughing fully for once. Granda danced with Gran, albeit more slowly, the two of them spinning in happy circles.

"A music box," Andrés said, staring with interest at the gilded cube. "I haven't seen one of those in ages. It must be ancient!"

Magical objects were relatively rare, the art of capturing magic in inanimate shapes having been forgotten long ago. Magic users were not all that common, but there were enough of them that every settlement boasted a few. Magical objects, though, were hardly an everyday occurrence.

"It's been in my family for probably six hundred years," I said. "The only magic we own. I think Papi took it in to be cleaned once and the magician nearly had a heart attack trying to get Papi to sell it to him."

"I can imagine," Andrés said, sipping on some wine and still staring at the box. "My father has a magic inkwell, but all it does is never run out of ink. Useful for all the paperwork he has to do, I guess, but not nearly as amazing as the music box."

Papi's playing slowed a bit, shifting from the more lively dance music into something soothing and lush. I smiled, sinking into the music.

"Do you want to dance?" Andrés held his hand

out to me. He was looking right at me, meeting my gaze even when I blinked and looked away. His smile was soft, warm, and something about it made my cheeks flush and my skin tingle. I gaped, not sure what to do.

"Dance with the man," Zapyros rumbled. His head lay on the patio stones just beyond the warming fires. His eyes drooped a little as though he were drowsing, but I knew he was paying attention. I felt a nudge of encouragement in my mind.

"Kayleigh is an *excellent* dancer," Mami said, waving her wine glass through the air in a flourish. She sighed. "She could have won over the hearts of any high society gathering if dancing were the only thing that mattered."

Now I was blushing in earnest, staring at the ground and desperately hoping that Andrés would chuckle and give up, yet also hoping he wouldn't.

"Then I really must dance with you," Andrés said. I lifted my eyes. He was still looking at me with that warm smile, his hand still extended. I took it, letting him pull me to my feet.

Marco stepped away from Carmen and took his turn with the guitar, plucking out the strains of a lively, dramatic waltz. The music box started playing a beat later, and then I was dancing. With Andrés.

Mami's praise of my dancing notwithstanding, I *was* quite good. I had often run around, channelling my energy to fly across the ground as swiftly as my legs would take me. But when I was forced to be inside, or when Mami had decided that I needed to learn how to fit into society, dancing had been my outlet. And so I mastered dance.

Andrés's arms were strong and sure, guiding me across the patio with relative ease. He didn't hesitate to hold me tight, just as I liked, and I found myself closing my eyes, falling away into the music and the dance. There, in that moment, turning and spinning and gliding my way across the makeshift dance floor in the arms of someone who held me just right, I found a different sort of flying. I realised then that when running, when dancing, any of it, I'd really been looking to fly all along.

The music ended and everyone clapped. I pulled back, sure that my face was bright red. Andrés held onto my hand, twining his fingers with mine. "They were right," he murmured as we took our seats again, just in time for Gran to demand her cake. "You dance spectacularly."

"Thank you," I said, and for the first time, I didn't feel like looking away.

I didn't dance any more that evening, though Andrés danced with Mami and Carmen both. He tried to convince Gran to take a turn with him, but she just blushed and claimed she was far too old for dancing. After a while, I slipped away from the patio full of lights and music, looking for somewhere quieter, my senses ready for peace.

I went through the back gate and into the bottom pasture, devoid of cattle for the evening and lit by the light of the moon. It was a familiar walk, one I'd taken may times as a child, but now it felt almost foreign. As if I hadn't been there in years, not a few months. I stumbled over a hole in the ground that I used to remember to leap over and decided that this sense of strangeness wasn't just because I hadn't been here for a bit. This place wasn't my home anymore.

I felt more comfortable in the Guild Hall, reading books in my quarters or eating meals in the dining hall, prepping Zapyros for riding, than I did on the farm where I'd grown up. It was nice to come back here, to visit, but I knew I wouldn't ever call this place home again, no matter what happened. A part of me was sad for it, and another part was ready to carve my own path.

I settled with my back against the low stone wall that bordered the bottom pasture, the hard surface softened by moss. The night was quiet, perfectly warm, and the light was not harsh enough to hurt my eyes. I let out a long breath and sank into relaxation.

Heavy footsteps startled me into awareness. Zapyros. I sat up and looked around, but the wardancer was on the other side of the wall, walking with someone else by his side. Andrés.

"It has gotten easier with Markham gone," Zapyros said in what sounded like a grudging admittance. "Without his...dissent, it is easier to be treated as just another courier dragon."

"They don't bother you?" Andrés sounded serious. I smiled to myself, secretly pleased at his concern for my dragon. It was something neither Zapyros nor I talked about much with each other, both of us being outsiders. Andrés, though, was on the inside, and his interest was touching. I ducked down further beneath the wall so they wouldn't see me.

"Why would they?" Zapyros rumbled. "I don't talk about Caspar Venir and they do not ask. To them, I am just a transport dragon, even if I am not bred for it. I...I fit in. Well, as much as I can, anyways."

Good. I was glad he fit in. Glad he felt comfortable in the Courier's Guild, after whatever horrible things he'd experienced at Caspar Venir, when he'd lost his previous rider.

"Let me know if you encounter any problems. I want to help," Andrés said. Zapyros hummed deep in his throat. There was silence for a minute, then, "I'm pretty certain her father said she came out here, but I can't see her."

"Let me try," Zapyros said. A moment later, there was a tapping on the wall in my mind. *Where are you, Little Bird?*

Nowhere, I replied even as I stood up and climbed over the wall towards them. "Did you enjoy the party?" I asked. Andrés smiled and nodded.

"I did. Thank you for inviting me. Based on your description, I half expected to have to fend of more flutterlings."

I snorted. "They were on their best behaviour for you, don't worry."

"It is getting late, Little Bird." Zapyros lowered his head to peer at me with a great amber eye. I rubbed the ridges above it and he leaned into the touch. "We had better get back."

"Yes. Pennytyne and I have a short route tomorrow, and then it's back to gathering supplies for the race. Can you believe it? Two more days and then we'll be flying across all of Amontyr!"

"At least you'll have decent competition," Zapyros grumbled. He stuck out his leg for Andrés and I to climb then took to the air with a frustrated snap of his wings.

"Zapyros is just upset that we're only technically competing against one other dragon," I explained. "Transport dragons are rare, after all."

"I could compete against the courier dragons," Zapyros complained, sparks trailing from his mouth. "I've half a mind to do so and prove everyone wrong about transport dragons."

"I'm sure Pennytyne would love to fly rings around you," Andrés laughed. "Couriers are bred for speed!"

"There's more to a race than speed, human, and I'll prove it."

Zapyros and Andrés bickered all the way back to the Guild Hall, leaving me content to sit in silence and smile.

CHAPTER 20

Because Ilisar was the largest city in western Amontyr, it was the designated location for the start of the Great Race. Over the next few days up until a day before race day, dragons flew in from all over Amontyr. The city's inns were all full and residents were renting out space in their homes to travellers come for the race. People wrote letters to be put into the official race bags and the number of people wearing courier blue went far beyond the usual Guild members.

On the morning of race day, I had already run a circuit around the small hill by the Guild Hall where the dragons roosted, just to get out my nervous energy. I wasn't the only one; Anna and Andrés had joined me at the start of my second circuit, their eyes bright and faces flushed with excitement. We were nothing, though, compared to our dragons.

"When will this event begin?" Zapyros demanded, pacing back and forth in the field outside the Hall. His claws dug furrows into the ground and the blades on his tail sheared off the grass. He was saddled and ready, and had been for nearly an hour, now.

"We have to wait for midday," I explained, not for the first time. "The first day is always the shortest, since they have to check every entrant to make sure that no one has entered illegally, that they're all cleared to fly, that they know the rules—"

"Yes, yes, I know!" Zapyros snapped. Sparks flew from his nostrils. Windcatcher, who had been wheeling around his head as if it were some great sport, flared her wings indignantly at the near-miss of a particularly large ember. She flew to Andrés and buried her head in his hair. Pennytyne, who was waiting sensibly and calmly, just snorted. Cyneric, sprawled out like some great cat surveying his territory, yawned, showing off his fangs.

"You're just wasting energy," he said, blinking blearily. "This is a *race*, after all. You'll need all the energy you can get."

Zapyros narrowed his eyes and opened his

mouth to growl something—probably something rude, knowing him—at the smaller dragon. I cleared my throat pointedly. He huffed, but settled into a low crouch, tail still twitching. Anna, hand shielding her eyes as she watched the new arrivals, snorted a laugh.

A shadow fell over the field where the racers waited, nearly blocking out the sun. I shielded my eyes and resisted the urge to let out a low whistle. "The other transport dragon is here."

"At last!" Zapyros rose to his feet again so he could get a proper measure of the newcomer. She landed heavily rather than gracefully, shoulders rolling with the jolt. Her scales were a deep shade of green with streaks of blue beneath her wings and her horns were little more than rounded nubs on her head. She was nearly as large as Zapyros, but where he was powerful muscle, she was stocky and bandylegged. Her wings were absolutely massive, though, like great sails meant to catch the wind and keep her aloft. I could see at once why the Guild would want such a dragon to transport crates and packages.

Zapyros nudged me with a claw. "Let's go!"

Before I could ask where, he was already striding off towards the transport dragon. I shot a look at

Andrés, who shrugged. Then, grumbling under my breath, I trudged after Zapyros.

"Good morrow," he said, far more formally than I'd ever heard. "I am Zapyros and this is my rider, Kayleigh Espinosa. I believe we are to be your competition in this race."

The transport dragon lifted her head from where she'd been conferring with her rider. She looked Zapyros over. Her lip curled, revealing the tips of her fangs. "Competition? Hardly. You're not a transport dragon. You could never even hope to match me or Victoire."

The rider, a tall woman with gleaming gold hair and blue eyes, pressed a hand to her dragon's shoulder. "Hush, Jasmine. It's not their fault that the Guild was desperate enough to recruit from, well, whatever they could get."

Rage ignited within me, sharp and hot. Zapyros's head reared back as though he'd been struck. He looked at me in alarm and confusion and I very nearly saw red. "I beg your pardon?" I asked, sure to keep my voice unflinchingly polite.

Victoire flashed a smile at me. "Oh, I don't mean any offence, I assure you. It's just that the sickness which felled so many of our transport dragons also means that the Guild was desperate.

I'm sure they were thrilled to recruit your, ah, dragon."

"Zapyros is a wardancer," I said in that same even tone, even as he shifted his weight. I'd never known him to be uncomfortable in the presence of others, but then, I'd also never met anyone stupid enough to speak badly to him to his face. "And we've been working transport for two months, now."

Victoire smiled sympathetically. "I'm sure. What did they promise you to get you to ride with him? Extra pay?"

I returned the smile, only this time with a dragon's show of fang. "Only the chance to trounce you in this race."

With that, I spun on my heel and walked away. Zapyros followed, a threatening growl rumbling deep in his chest. By the time we made it back to our friends, I was fuming.

"What happened?" Andrés asked. "Did you speak with Rider Victoire?"

"We spoke," I hissed. "She all but called Zapyros useless!"

"It wasn't like that," Zapyros said. "She only said that I'm not bred for transport work." His voice was steady, but in my mind, I could feel the riot of emotions spilling over the bond. He was hurt.

Unsure. We had both faced our share of bias and prejudice, but no one had been as openly rude as that rider and her dragon.

"That is not what she said and you know it." I rounded on my dragon and jabbed him in the arm with a finger. He recoiled, wide-eyed, tail twitching. "And we're going to beat those two soundly, do you hear me?"

In an instant, he puffed up with pride and eagerness. "It would be my pleasure, Little Bird."

Zapyros roared, the sound rattling the stones on the ground and drawing the attention of every person and dragon in the field. I saw Jasmine pull back, flaring her wings in discomfort, and wasn't displeased with the result, not at all.

"Alright, alright, that's enough of that!" An official from the Guild emerged into the sunlight, carrying a stack of papers. They were accompanied by Master Templeton and wearing the same robes denoting administrator rank. "My name is Flavius Barrow, head of the courier and transport dragon division of the Guild. Riders, dragons, listen and listen well. These are the rules for the race, and if you break them, your entry is forfeit."

I leaned forward on my toes to get a better look. Zapyros hooked his claws around me and lifted me to his back, but his attention also never strayed from Guildmaster Barrow.

"The Great Race will depart midday from Ilisar and follow the pre-determined route across Amontyr. Each dragon, courier or transport class, will be carrying either a bag of letters or a crate of goods, depending on their class. These items must be carried through the entire race, intact, and given for delivery at the end of the race. There will be rest points along the way where you may stay at the end of a day's flying, free of charge, but the same rules apply to the letters or crates as apply to any delivery in the Guild: they must not be out of a rider's view for fear of tampering. You will fly from sunup to sundown. There will be no night flying. There will be no sabotaging another rider and dragon. No fighting with each other. If you encounter difficulties along the way and require medical attention, then you will find it at any of the rest points. You may forfeit at any time. During the duration of the race, all participants are exempt from their normal courier duties and may not be flagged down for delivering of post. Do you understand these rules?"

"Yes, Guildmaster!" The cry rang out across the field.

The Guildmaster nodded and tucked his list of

rules into his robes. "Well, what are you waiting for? Let's get to the starting point!"

There was chaos in the field for a minute as riders mounted their dragons and everyone flew or ran to cross the river. Zapyros merely spread his wings halfway and leaped over, landing neatly on the other side and twitching his hide like a cat. I would have bet several gold coins that Jasmine was watching.

The bags of letters were handed out and Jasmine and Zapyros were given medium-sized crates. I latched it down securely and covered it with oilcloth, just in case.

"Are you ready, Little Bird?" Zapyros asked. I strapped myself into the saddle, pulled on my flight goggles, put my ear muffs on, and watched the Guildmaster eagerly.

"Ready," I called across our mental bond.

The Guildmaster raised a flag in courier blue. Zapyros crouched. The flag dropped.

"Let's fly!"

CHAPTER 21

Zapyros leaped into the air with a single beat of his wings. It was a testament to his strength that he managed to pull into the heights of the sky within a few moments, moving swiftly enough to have my stomach in my throat. The smaller courier dragons were in the sky nearly as quickly as Zapyros, darting in all directions to avoid fouling on each other's wings. The transport dragon was the slowest of them all, taking a few leaping jumps with her wings pumping before they finally caught on the wind and took her into the sky.

Zapyros snorted in satisfaction, sparks floating through the air. He circled the Guild Hall once, drinking in the cheers of onlookers, before turning to the north and leaving Ilisar behind. I kept an eye out for

Andrés and Anna, and when each winged by on Penny-tyne and Cyneric, I greeted them with a wave. Wind-catcher was perched on Pennytyne's saddle, maw open to the wind as if she were roaring with excitement.

The courier dragons were, generally, much faster than the larger transport dragon or Zapyros. Their small size made it possible for them to dart in and out of a place, delivering messages with speed. They were more manoeuvrable and in the short term, they could easily beat Zapyros in a race. The trick, though, was in endurance. After the initial burst of speed, most of the courier dragons slowed consider-ably, their wings beating slowly and steadily to get them through the long-distance race.

Zapyros, too, was faster than Jasmine in the short term. We easily outpaced Jasmine and Victoire within the first few minutes, until they were a decently large smudge of colour behind us. The question was whether we would be able to match the enduring power of those sail-like wings that Jasmine boasted.

"She'll be weighed down by her bulk, but if she can climb high enough, she might be able to glide for a good portion of the day, where we'll have to stop and rest," I said through our mental bridge. Zapyros huffed and

didn't respond except to angle his own ascent higher and beat his wings a little faster. "*Whatever happened to you claiming that you could fly for two days without stop?*"

"*I wasn't lying,*" he protested. "*Only, if I can fly that long and far, so can she. If I fly higher and faster, then I can go farther than she can just gliding.*"

I didn't remind Zapyros that we would be required to stop at the end of each day. He knew the rules. It would be useless trying to get any conversation out of him besides the strategic flying and speculation on our opponent. Instead, I pulled out my notebook and made notes on our relative position based on the angle of the sun and landmarks on the ground. It wasn't quite the same as drawing the map in full, but at this speed there wasn't much point in even trying.

We flew without slowing or stopping until the sun started towards the horizon and I spotted the flags of the first town and rest point. Zapyros turned towards it and landed neatly in a field on the outskirts of town. There were several courier dragons here already, including Pennytyne, looking as though they had been here a while. I didn't see Cyneric's distinctive red scales, though. Zapyros narrowed his eyes at the smaller dragons. His breath was even, but heavy, and I frowned.

"You pushed yourself too hard today. They'll be stopping here, too, remember."

He just rolled his shoulders and growled slightly, startling the runner that had emerged from the town. The boy was perhaps fourteen and stared at Zapyros with wide, horrified eyes.

"Rider Kayleigh Espinosa and Zapyros, reporting for the end of the first day of the Great Race," I said coldly. The runner snapped his jaw shut.

"Right. Yes. Of course. Um, Dwerheven welcomes you to the first rest stop and offers you accommodations in our finest inn, The Dancing Mule. If you'll please follow me, Rider."

"I cannot," I said. "I am not to leave my cargo unattended, so will be spending the night here. With Zapyros."

The runner squawked in shock. "But...but you have to! We're supposed to offer free accommodations and food and—"

"She stays here with me," Zapyros said, showing a fang. The boy shut up, growing pale. "You may bring food for both my rider and myself. A cow, I think, would be quite satisfactory. Roasted and salted."

"A *whole* cow?" The boy looked like he might faint.

"Yes. Is that a problem?" Zapyros lowered his head so that he was staring the boy in the face. The boy spluttered denial, then agreement, and finally raced off back to Dwerheven.

"A whole cow, really?" I gathered my pack and slid from Zapyros's back before he could lower himself to the ground. He grumbled. "You ate a sheep last night. Did you really fly hard enough to warrant a cow?"

"Perhaps not, but I am hungry, and we were promised free food, were we not?" Zapyros settled in like a cat and started licking at the scales on his foot.

"And if you're too weighed down to outrace Jasmine?"

"As if a measly cow could weigh me down that much." My comment had sparked a light of unease in Zapyros's eyes. He shook his great head and went back to grooming his claws. "I'll just be able to fly longer, that's all. And I can go without food tomorrow."

I snorted. "I thought you military types were very particular about eating proper rations and doing things to ensure fighting fitness, not demanding ridiculous provisions from terrified villagers."

That, it would appear, was the wrong thing to say. Zapyros reared his head back and hissed at me, eyes narrowed. "You know *nothing* of what it is like to be in the military. To dedicate your entire existence to the art of war. Do not presume to preach to me about such matters, human."

I flinched and immediately lowered my gaze. "Sorry," I said quickly. "I didn't mean...I was only teasing."

He growled once and turned his head from me, laying it on the ground. I shifted my weight, trying to come up with a proper apology, a way to make things right, to unsay what I foolishly said. Finally, I settled for, "I'm going to go on a quick run, stretch my legs."

Zapyros blew some sparks from his nose, but didn't respond. So I took off, jogging lightly before settling into my run, legs eating up the ground so that the world around me blurred into vague shapes and colours. I'd never been to Dwerheven, and it was barely a dot on my maps, but somehow it looked and felt too much like home. The trees, the fields, it was too familiar. My throat tightened, and I ran faster, seized by a need to be somewhere else. Anywhere else.

I was such an idiot.

How could I say such things to Zapyros, knowing that he'd lost his first rider during his service, that he'd only transferred away from the Aerial Corps because it was too painful for him to be there. Yet I'd casually said those things because, what, I thought it was funny to tease him about his past?

I slowed and stopped, blinking back tears. Somehow I'd found myself at the field again, only now it was populated with several more dragons, including Jasmine. Pennytyne had moved to where Zapyros was resting. Most of the smaller couriers had made it and were settling down into groups, their riders talking with smiles and hand movements, doing nothing but conferring about the first day of the race as they headed to the inn for the night. Even more than before, I felt out of place. A desire to be anywhere else. To spare others my inability to fit in.

"Kayleigh!" Andrés jogged up to me, his face windblown from a day's riding. He must have been checking in at the inn, because he looked as fresh as when we'd started the day, whereas I was a sweaty mess. I flushed. "How long have you and Zapyros been here? I wasn't sure we'd see you tonight."

"About an hour or so?" I'd lost track of time while running, as I usually did. "He pushed himself hard today."

Andrés chuckled. "I'm not surprised. Pennytyne wanted to do the same thing, but I reminded her that we were all likely to end up at the rest point regardless. It'll be the next few days where we see real progress in those that can't manage the long-distance flying over several days. Do you think that it will be long before we outpace you and Zapyros? Pennytyne was anxious about it all day. She wants so badly to prove how fast she is to him."

I hummed acknowledgement, but my thoughts were anywhere but the race. "Oh, look, I think that's people with Zapyros's dinner. I'd better go direct them."

I hurried off to where several villagers where wheeling in a wagon with a roasted cow, eyeing the hungry gazes of the small dragons with alarm. Dwerheven must not have all that many dragons of their own to be so concerned with less than fifty. I caught up with the wagon and pointed to Zapyros, who was now sitting with head up in a regal posture, talking with Pennytyne and Cyneric, who looked like he'd just arrived. Windcatcher rested on his head, her claws gripping one of his horns as he talked.

"Yes, we got here quite early," Zapyros said, sniffing. "I'm surprised that you weren't here already when we landed, given how swiftly you flew off this morning."

"We stopped for a rest at midday," Cyneric said. "Anna insisted, so that I wouldn't strain myself on the first day."

"Andrés thought we should, too, but I overruled him. He says that—is that a cow?" Pennytyne swung her head over and sniffed eagerly. The villagers baulked.

"Here you are, Zapyros," I said, thanking them. The villagers ran off, only too eager to get away from dragons at mealtime. "*I am sorry,*" I said through the bond. The wall in my mind seemed especially thick, but a trickle of confusion reached me and made me flinch. "*I didn't mean to bring up…any of it. I just—*"

"Enough, Little Bird," Zapyros said aloud. "You apologised already. and I forgive you. It is forgotten." He nuzzled me gently before turning to his cow.

"That's…it?" I had expected chastising, silent fuming, even.

Zapyros froze, jaws inches from his dinner. "Did you mean to cause pain?"

"No! Of course not!"

He smiled, and this time his nuzzle was not so gentle. "Then yes, that's it. Now, are you going to let me eat or not?"

My shoulders suddenly felt light. I smiled, relieved, and took the tray of my own food from the wagon. We ate around a small fire that Zapyros had created while most of the riders went off to The Dancing Mule for their own supper and rooms. A few stayed in the field with their dragons, including Victoire, who set up a tent besides Jasmine with a glare in our direction. I hadn't bothered to set up the tent; Zapyros produced enough heat the with the fires in his belly, and with a wing stretched over me, I was perfectly safe and secure from any potential weather.

A bright flash of light woke me in the middle of the night. I scrambled out from under the deep blue wing, careful not to snag the membranes in case I woke Zapyros. I needn't have feared. He was awake, nose pointed towards the horizon, eyes narrowed. The other dragons, too, were awake, rumbling amongst themselves.

"What's going on?" I asked, speech slurred by sleep.

Another flash of light filled the sky, nearly blinding me.

"A storm is moving in." Zapyros's voice was solemn. My mouth grew dry. The Great Race made no provisions for weather, as couriers were charged with delivering the post no matter the conditions, unless their own life was at stake. By tomorrow, that storm would be here, and we would have to fly through it.

CHAPTER 22

By morning, the storm had hit with a howling vengeance. Several courier dragons and their riders withdrew from the race when one of the trees bordering the field fell over from the force of the wind. The rain was sharp and piercingly cold and lightning and thunder shook the sky periodically.

"Are you sure it's safe to fly through this?" I asked Zapyros when a particularly violent lightning strike had thunder chasing it before the light had even faded. "Lightning is dangerous, surely, even to dragons."

"To some, yes," Zapyros said, glaring at the sky, "but many dragons have a mineral in their scales that grounds the electricity. It's not the same as the resistance that many stormchaser dragons have, but it will keep us safe."

Which meant we were still in the race.

"What about you?" I asked Andrés and Anna. They were wearing coats made of oilcloth lined with fur, but they already looked miserable. Their saddles weren't big enough for them to huddle under a makeshift shelter, like mine was. They would be facing the full brunt of the storm.

"We will fly," Cyneric said, lashing his tail at a particularly strong burst of rain. He bared his teeth and growled. "No storm is going to subdue me."

Anna looked less certain, but she lay her hand on Cyneric's leg and nodded. "We'll fly."

Andrés exchanged a look with Zapyros, who tossed his head. Pennytyne stretched her wings and squeaked when another flash of lightning lit the sky. "I am capable of flying through lightning," she said warily, "but this wind is likely to blow us off course."

Zapyros hummed, the sound deep in his chest, his claws working the ground uneasily. I hadn't considered that. The smaller dragons were capable fliers, but this wind was strong and relentless, blowing the rain sideways. It would easily throw them around like ragdolls.

"You will fly behind us," my dragon announced

at last. "I can create a wedge through the wind, and you will be less likely to be tossed about."

"We don't need help!" Cyneric protested. Anna scoffed.

"Yes," she said firmly, "we do. Or have you forgotten the flutterling incident already? This is worse than that."

The red dragon huffed, and didn't argue. Andrés shrugged, though he looked concerned. Wind-catcher poked her head out of the front of his jacket and shivered before pulling herself back inside. Maybe this race wasn't a good idea. No. I shook my head. We were couriers. Regardless of whether we were trying to win a race, we would deliver the post in any weather. This was just a way to prove it. To everyone.

"So long as you're sure," I said, but I was already climbing into the saddle and checking the oilcloth over the crates we were carrying. I buckled myself into the seat, pulling an oilcloth over my own head and securing it down to loops meant to hold additional supplies.

"*Ready*," I said, mentally tapping at the wall in my mind twice. Zapyros let out a defiant roar, flame painting the sky nearly as brightly as the lightning. Beside us, Pennytyne and Cyneric spread their wings and roared their own defiance, Andrés and Anna whooping into the might of the storm.

Zapyros crouched and leaped into the sky, wings beating heavily to fight against the wind. The two courier dragons followed closely in our wake. We were three amongst ten that had taken to the skies that morning, out of nearly forty riders and dragons. Jasmine and Victoire climbed into the sky a few moments after us, the transport dragon's massive wings straining as the wind caught in them and tried to pull her off course. Her bulk worked in her favour though, for she was too heavy to be swept away and instead bulled her way through the storm.

"Change your heading two points north," I thought, studying the ground beneath us. It was beginning to blur from the rain all around, but there was enough detail for me to know exactly where we were and where we needed to be. For the first time since bonding with Zapyros, I wished heartily to be studying the route from the safety and warmth of my room, map spread on a table instead of in my mind, blurred by rain and lightning.

Zapyros shifted his flying without question and then we fought our way into the heart of a storm.

The dragons flew closer to the ground, hoping to avoid some of the winds that were likely to toss them around at higher altitudes. Even through the thick saddle leather, I could feel Zapyros constantly shifting his wings and body to counter the storm. Lightning occasionally illuminated the sky, but it didn't get close enough to strike us, for which I was extremely grateful. I didn't want to experience being struck by lightning, even if what Zapyros said was true.

About an hour into the flight, we winged past Jasmine, her own massive wings fighting desperately to keep her heading forwards. I shifted in my saddle, watching her flight.

"Surely if she flies across the wind instead of against it, she'll move faster," I thought to Zapyros. We were constantly scuttling across the wind, first one direction and then another, keeping on course and making it as easy as possible. Jasmine, though, looked to be fighting it head on.

"Yes, but then she'll have to spend extra time making up the distance to reach the second checkpoint and probably fly twice as far. With her wings, flying like we are will take her wildly off course. It's a matter of choosing the most efficient path," Zapyros barely spared a glance at the struggling transport dragon as we inched our way past her. He did, I note, swing his head around every few minutes to make sure that

Cyneric and Pennytyne were still in our wake. I started doing the same, even though it earned me a face full of rain every time I did.

The smaller courier dragons were obviously struggling, taking two beats of their wings for every one of Zapyros's, but they kept up admirably, flying in formation without any issue. I guessed all that extra training in formation flying those first weeks were actually working in our favour, for once. Not that I was likely to write a thank you note to Markham and Clover.

The storm eventually slowed, the lightning fading into nothingness and the rain becoming little more than a light drizzle that made Zapyros's scales gleam in the half-light. The wind, though, remained. Worse, it became unsteady, blowing in swift gusts that threatened to throw us off course, then falling aside abruptly, making the dragons struggle to right themselves. After three hours of this, I could tell that even Zapyros's seemingly endless stamina was flagging.

"We have to stop. Take a break."

"Just a little farther, Little Bird. I think I see a village up ahead." Zapyros beat his wings harder, and I strained to see what his superior eyes had caught.

The wind that we'd been fighting for the last

several minutes dropped off precipitously. Zapyros growled as his muscles strained to turn his wings and keep him flying straight and true. If I hadn't been buckled in, I was certain that I would have been sliding about. I checked behind to make sure that the crates were still secure. Then, I saw Penny-tyne wobble.

"Pennytyne!" I called. The green dragon strained her wings, but she had reached the end of her ability. She faltered. Her left wing didn't beat in the same cadence with her right. Cyneric tried to shore her up by flying beneath her so that the updraft might steady her, but it was too late. In an instant, Pennytyne started falling from the sky. Andrés met my eyes with blind panic written plainly across his features.

"*Zapyros!*" I screamed both mentally and out loud, pushing against the wall with all my might in my desperate urgency. In an instant, the wall between us shattered. I could see the world through Zapyros's eyes as clearly as if they'd been my own. The colours shifted and blurred as he spun, folding his wings tightly against him. Determination warred with horror and we spiralled towards the falling dragon.

Pennytyne beat her wings desperately. No

matter how she fought, the gusting wind and her own exhaustion seemed to battle against her. She continued to fall. Cyneric screeched, circling high above us. I could feel Zapyros pull his wings in tighter, tucking his legs as though they were my legs, using our tail as a rudder to steer us close to the flailing Pennytyne.

"*Brace yourself*," he said, the words echoing across the shining bridge that lay between our minds. Emotion swirled between us freely and my panic was drowned out by his determination, his need to get there in time this time.

This time.

Images swam in my head, making my heart beat faster. Another manoeuvre over snow-capped mountains. An attack, wardancer fighting rival wardancer and other smaller combat dragons. No time to gear up properly. Just a hiss at my rider and a leap into the sky. And then a dragon flamed me. I spun, and my rider screamed. Falling, falling. He hadn't been paying attention, too distracted to hold on. I dove. He fell. I was too slow.

Zapyros's wings snapped open in an instant, pulling me from the images in my mind. Memories, I understood in that brief moment before Pennytyne crashed into Zapyros's back, her claws digging into saddle and scale to right herself. Zapyros let out a roar, wings straining as he took the weight of the smaller dragon.

"Land!" Andrés was screaming at me. I could barely think straight with all this new emotion flooding me, but through this new bridge of ours, Zapyros heard us. He banked, hard, heading to the ground too fast.

A meadow full of wildflowers opened up before us. Zapyros fell to the ground, impacting like a meteor in a crater. He slid on the ground, wings scraping over grass and rock. Pennytyne tumbled from his back, landing hard on her shoulder, one wing bent awkwardly beneath her. The world was full of motion and shifting colours and then suddenly, it was quiet.

"Little Bird?" Zapyros croaked. I blinked dirt out of my eyes. My ears rang, and I scrabbled at my earmuffs, the thought of wearing them for a moment longer suddenly unbearable. I pulled off my goggles and my hat, started in on the buckles. "Kayleigh!"

I started. The wall in my mind was back, though I could tell it was a wobbly, weak thing that I'd thrown up in my own defence so I wouldn't be over-whelmed by the noise, the emotion, the memories. I made a sound that could barely be identified as a word.

"Are you alright?" Zapyros asked, lifting his head to peer at me.

"Yes," I confirmed, though I wasn't sure whether I was lying or telling the truth. I wasn't hurt physically, I didn't think, though I was extremely sore. "You?"

"I'll live." He struggled to his feet and stretched his wings once before folding them in on themselves. I saw a few small holes in the delicate membrane, but there were no obvious breaks. Not like Pennytyne.

"Pennytyne! Andrés!" I scrabbled at the buckles on the saddle, practically sliding to the ground. I stumbled my way to where the smaller courier dragon was. A moment later and Cyneric landed, Anna already in the process of dismounting. We ran to Pennytyne.

"Andrés?"

He was still buckled into his own saddle and there was a nasty cut on his head where it looked like he'd scraped it against a rock or something. But he was blinking up at me, smiling weakly. "Kayleigh," he said. "You're alright."

A shadow fell over my shoulder. Andrés's eyes

watered as he looked up at Zapyros. "You came for me."

"Of course I did," my dragon snapped. He reached up with a talon and practically sliced Andrés from the saddle. Andrés groaned, but stood with no apparent issue. He unzipped his jacket and Windcatcher crawled out, her whole body trembling.

"Hey," Andrés said, nuzzling her head. "You're alright. Go with Kayleigh, would you? I need to check on Pennytyne."

The harrier dragon leaped to my shoulders, wrapping her tail around my neck and burying her head in my hair. I lay a hand on her side, but I was too busy watching Pennytyne to do much more than provide a steady perch for the little dragon.

Pennytyne moaned. "Andrés?" she asked. He went to her head and lay a hand on her jaw.

"I'm okay. You did it."

"My wing hurts," she whimpered. Zapyros reared back on his hind legs and used his forelegs to lift her out of the awkward position she'd landed in. Pennytyne yelped and flinched as her injured side was shifted. Her right shoulder looked swollen, and there was blood oozing from a large gash across the muscle. Worse than that, though, was the way her right wing lay limp on the ground. Bent in a way that it should not bend.

Andrés hugged Pennytyne closely. "Don't look. It's going to be okay."

She looked anyways and her keening could be heard even over the screams of the wind. There was no way she would be able to fly in time to finish the Great Race. It would take months before she might be able to fly properly again. She might be able to fly faster if a healer with actual magic could work on her, but until then, she was grounded.

Acting on instinct, I stumbled over to Andrés and wrapped my arms tightly around him, holding him just how I would want to be held. He sagged against me and shook.

CHAPTER 23

It turned out that dragons crash landing in a field was a great way to draw attention. Within twenty minutes, several people from the town—Varwold—had appeared in the field with medical supplies, a few wide-eyed stragglers in tow. The healers were working on Andrés and Pennytyne within moments, and while none of them were magical, they were obviously quite capable.

"What of you?" a healer with a wry smile asked, wrinkles etching lines in her warm brown skin. She eyed me and Zapyros with a knowing look. "Your wings have holes in them."

Zapyros huffed, sparks drifting from his nose. "They are hardly anything to be concerned with. They will heal in a few days."

"I imagine they would heal better if you removed yourself from the race." The healer walked over to the wardancer as though he were a puppy, tapping him on the wing and humming over the scrapes on his hide where Pennytyne had dug her claws in.

Zapyros growled. "I finish things I start."

"A good philosophy, but you *are* bleeding." The healer held out her hand and, with a grumble, Zapyros lowered himself to the ground so she could climb his back. She leaned over each scratch, dabbing them with a cream of some sort.

"Are you sure you're alright, Little Bird?" he asked me for the fifth time, laying his head on the ground and taking me in. I tried not to sway where I stood, but gravity took over and suddenly I found myself sitting with my back against Zapyros's warm neck, my fingers picking at a trailing thread on my trousers.

"Um...when Pennytyne fell, something happened," I said, not quite sure how to articulate it. "The wall..."

"Fell." Zapyros sighed. Pennytyne yelped as the two healers at her wing set the bone. Andrés flinched, but he kept by Pennytyne's side, murmuring to her. Anna and Cyneric watched from a distance, the red dragon flicking his wings in discomfort. "Yes. It...it can happen when a soul-bonded pair experiences extreme emotion. The walls that keep our thoughts separate and our minds whole, they collapse. What happens next is a sort of melding. Two becomes one. It's extremely dangerous because it's so easy to get lost in the other's thoughts. There are stories of riders and dragons who forsake the walls entirely and act as one entity in two bodies."

I shuddered. "That sounds horrific." Then, because that sounded meaner than I intended, "Not that I think sharing your thoughts is a bad thing, it's just—"

Zapyros chuckled. "I understand, Little Bird. I, too, enjoy having my own mind."

I picked at the trailing thread again. "When, uh, our thoughts were merged, I saw a...a memory."

The warmth at my back disappeared as Zapyros lifted his head and studied the clouds. If dragons could cry, I was certain he would be. Instead, he just sort of huddled in on himself, his wings pulled tight against his body, his tail curling around his legs. "Garret was many things—brave, intelligent, kind—but he was also careless. He knew that we were often called into battle at a moment's notice, and that the most important thing was to secure himself to the saddle so we could fight. More than that, to pay attention to what I was doing and hold on. He...I wasn't fast enough."

"I'm so sorry." I lay a hand on Zapyros's leg, tracing my thumb over the hard ridges of his scales. "I saw it. You did everything you could. It was an accident."

He sighed. "I tried to go back to being a soldier, a warrior, after that, but I couldn't. I'd lost all taste for combat. And the skirmishes along the mountain border were ending, anyways, with the new treaty between Synval and Drimior so I decided to try something different. Something without any fighting."

"Well, I'm glad you chose to be a courier," I murmured. "If it matters."

To my utter surprise, Zapyros turned and nudged me, his massive head nearly knocking me over. "It matters a great deal."

We camped that night in the meadow, provided with food for everyone from the generosity of the villagers. The food in the more northern climes was distinctly less spiced and flavourful than I was used to, but made up for it with a richness that filled the belly quite nicely. I ate two bowls of the beef stew with root vegetables, mopping up the last bits with a roll of crusty bread. Anna and Cyneric ate with gusto, as did Pennytyne. Even Zapyros crunched on a goat, though he'd eaten that cow yesterday.

Andrés, though, merely stirred his stew with his spoon and stared into the fire.

"What's wrong?" I asked, shifting to sit closer to him.

"Nothing."

I quirked a brow. "I may be completely inept at most social interactions, but I'd have to be entirely blind and deaf to not know that you're lying."

Andrés smiled weakly. "Yeah, alright."

"Is it the race?"

He shrugged. "I just...I really thought I had a chance at winning, you know? We're so fast. And Pen, she has so much more endurance than most other couriers, so I figured the long distance part of the race would be fairly easy for us. You know?"

"I'm sorry," Pennytyne said, snaking her head over and nuzzling Andrés on the cheek. Her eyes welled as if with tears, though dragons could not cry. "It's all my fault."

"It is not!" Andrés gaped up at his dragon. "Nothing about that was your fault. You flew valiantly!"

"Indeed," Cyneric said, licking his talons. "If I were as small as you, I would have easily been taken by the wind."

"It was *my* fault," Zapyros said. I was about to protest when he shot me a warning glance. "*Let them have someone to blame. My shoulders are strong enough.*"

I kept silent, but a warmth spread in my heart. I was bonded to a kind dragon.

"If I had not insisted on flying so far, not taking into account your potential difficulties with the storm, then we none of us would have crashed. I should have been more considerate, and for that I apologise." Zapyros lowered his head. Pennytyne hesitated.

"It is over and done with," she said at last. Windcatcher, perched on Pennytyne's shoulder, rubbed her head against the green dragon's hide. "I am only sorry you have to give up the race for me," she said to Andrés.

"No one could have predicted that storm." He smiled up at his dragon. "If it hadn't been for that, we would have taken the trophy without contest."

I hummed in agreement. Pennytyne was fairly strong and her endurance was quite impressive. Even Cyneric, who was bigger than the green courier, couldn't match her distance flying. "You have to drop out because of an accident. You'll fly again, and then you'll be back to being a courier. No one will think less of you for this."

"Not in the Guild, perhaps." Andrés gave up on eating his stew and set the bowl on the ground. Windcatcher pounced, immediately sticking her head into the bowl and slurping it down in an extremely undignified manner. I bit back a laugh, but Andrés only watched. "My family."

"Ah." I was all too familiar with disappointing family.

"My father didn't want me joining the Guild. He wanted something more prestigious. Politics, or studying the law, or even serving in one of the great academies doing research. You know, something with power behind it." Andrés hunched his shoulders. "I just wanted to be out there, seeing the world and doing my best to make people happy. What could be better than delivering the post? Handing people letters from family or friends, seeing their face light up with good news. I know there's bad news in there, too, but I always loved getting the post as a kid. It's what I wanted."

Tentatively, I threaded my arm through his and lay my head on his shoulder. He didn't pull away, just held tighter. It wasn't the most comfortable touch for me, but I didn't want to retreat. I pressed my side against his. Better. "You thought that if you won the Great Race, your father would approve of your chosen career?"

Andrés nodded. "It's silly. It doesn't matter what my father thinks. I'm a courier, now, and I'm happy."

"That is important," I agreed. "But...maybe we don't stop wanting our family's approval?"

Pennytyne rested her head on the ground near Andrés. He scratched her eye ridges absently. "You have my approval, Andrés Mierza," Pennytyne murmured. "No matter what happens."

He took a deep breath and let it out slowly. "That means more than you could possibly know."

Windcatcher finished with the stew and sat grooming her scales like a cat, the fire reflecting off of her and making her gleam in the dark. "What about you? How far ahead do you think Jasmine and Victoire are? Do you think you still have a chance?"

"Of course we have a chance!" I glared at the fire.

"I doubt very much that they made it much farther than we did," Zapyros chimed in, his great head appearing over us as he dropped another log onto the fire. "Even with her size, the wind was too strong for her wings, I imagine. The wind didn't die down until an hour ago. She'll have been grounded, just like us. If we fly hard and fast tomorrow, we can make it to the second and third checkpoints. I may not be as fast as Pennytyne or Cyneric, but I have no doubt I'm faster than Jasmine." He sniffed disdainfully.

The storm had cleared entirely, and while I wasn't massively optimistic about our chances, nor did I want to give in. Like Andrés, I felt like I had something to prove. Not to my family, necessarily, though it would be nice to see the beaming pride on my mother's face. No, I wanted to do this for everyone who thought that neither Zapyros nor I belonged.

"We'll leave at first light," I declared. Zapyros growled in agreement.

"Cyneric and I will go, too," Anna said from across the fire. She sat with her arms folded around her middle, but there was a spark of determination in her eyes that was nothing to do with the reflection from the fire. "I doubt any of the other courier dragons made it very far in that storm. We only made it this far because of Zapyros, and there weren't any following in Jasmine's wake. Frankly, we're probably the farthest ahead. And with our speed, we'll definitely win!"

Andrés grinned. "Yes. You win this thing and show everyone how it's done."

Cyneric roared, puffing out his chest. Zapyros joined in. Livestock in the fields surrounding Varwold started making noise, and I heard the familiar barking roars of livestock dragons. "Goodness," I said. "You're setting everyone off. Maybe we'd better go to bed before we get a visit from the whole village."

Anna laughed. "No arguments here!" She stretched and went to her blanket, laid out on the ground next to her dragon.

"Certainly I could use some sleep," Andrés said, and I noticed just how tired he looked. Without thinking, I lifted my hand and traced the line of the cut across his forehead. He didn't flinch away, just caught my wrist and held me close.

"Kayleigh?"

"Yeah?"

"Win this thing," Andrés whispered. Then, in a movement I never expected, he brought his lips to mine. A brush, a whisper of a touch, then more firmly. I'd never been kissed before, but somehow I knew exactly what to do. How to open to him, how to move with him. How to start mingling my heart with his. What I didn't know was what to do after he pulled away, thumb brushing my cheek.

"What was that for?" I blurted out, glad for the light of the fire that would surely hide my blush.

"For good luck, of course," Andrés murmured. He smiled. "Perhaps you need some more."

"Maybe I do."

He kissed me again. And again. And again, until I went to sleep staring up at the sky and holding my fingers to my mouth, unable to bite back a smile.

CHAPTER 24

The next day dawned bright and clear with not a hint of cloud or wind to mar the sky. Zapyros was itching to go as soon as the sun crested the horizon and wasted no time in nudging me to my feet. He hovered over me while I packed my bags and nearly snapped Cyneric's head off when the red dragon announced that he and Anna were ready to fly.

"Good luck," Andrés said, squeezing my hand. "We'll see you at the finish line, yeah?"

"Where will you go?" I leaned towards him, not quite sure where this need to be close to him came from. I'd never been kissed before, sure, but was this after effect normal? Was wanting to just be tethered to him by a touch, a look, normal?

"Pen and I will travel to the river and then hire a barge to take us back to Ilisar." Andrés smiled at Pennytyne, who was resting with her head on the ground, looking listless. "It'll be a week's extra travel, but we'll get there."

"Take care of yourselves," I murmured.

"You, too." Andrés kissed my cheek, gently, softly, and then pulled back. "You'd better go before Zapyros leaves without you."

Zapyros snorted. "I would never."

"Yes, you would, now let me up." I climbed into the saddle and buckled myself in, announcing myself secure through our bond and receiving a pulse of relief in return. Zapyros snapped his wings open and beat them hard, lifting us into the air. Cyneric followed, circling the meadow once and letting out a triumphant roar before changing his heading and flying off.

Zapyros huffed, merely flicking his tail at Andrés and Pennytyne, blowing sparks at Windcatcher as she danced through the air beneath us. Then, he, too changed his heading and started towards the horizon.

Cyneric outflew us for the first part of the morning, straining his wings to his top speed until he was long out of view. I knew he'd have to rest before long, but he and Anna would at least make the second checkpoint by midday. Instead of going for speed, Zapyros settled into a steady rhythm, his wings beating so regularly that I had to start humming a song to keep from going mad with the noise.

We flew all day without pause, Zapyros even swooping down to scoop up mouthfuls of water from a small lake as we went. I ate food from my pack and updated the log and map I was keeping, eventually falling into a sleepless daze watching the landscape go by. Occasionally, I recognised a landmark enough to correct Zapyros's direction, but that was rare.

"*Second checkpoint ahead,*" I said just after the sun hit its zenith. Zapyros swooped lower, his wings nearly brushing the tops of the roofs of the farming town of Resi. People let out shouts of alarm—or cheers at our arrival—but Zapyros didn't stop, instead turning from the coast and heading inland towards our next checkpoint.

"*Shouldn't we have stopped? Checked in?*"

Zapyros grumbled. "*And lose more time? We don't know if Jasmine has already been here, but I'm not taking a chance. Besides, I got close enough for their couriers to mark who we are. There are only two trans-*

port class dragons in this race and if they don't know me, then they're fools. They can take down the information. I will keep flying."

And he did.

We reached the third checkpoint, Northcross, as the sun fell beneath the horizon, stopping only because the rules dictated we do so. There was no sign of Jasmine or Victoire, but we did see Anna and Cyneric in the field as we landed in the twilight gloom.

"Any news?" I asked when Anna stumbled towards our fire. She looked exhausted and was definitely walking stiffly. Long days in the saddle for her were far more uncomfortable than they were for me, given the size of her saddle. I winced on her behalf.

"We saw two other courier dragons on our way here, though I don't know if they made it here. No sign of Jasmine." Anna sat down carefully and pulled off her boots, groaning. "Today's flight was hard. Not just for me. Cyneric says that he thinks you'll start overtaking us soon. Four straight days of flying is about all we can manage. We'll have to start taking longer breaks. You'd think that we would be so much faster than you, that we'd always beat you to the finish line, but it's just not meant to be." She sighed dramatically and flopped onto her back. I laughed at the theatrics.

I'd always known that the Great Race was going to divide us at some point. Courier dragons weren't meant for long distance flying. They could outfly us in the short term with ease. As the flights grew longer, though, Zapyros's endurance would win the day. That was why the Courier Guild had so many more courier dragons than transport class ones; they needed to fly faster over shorter distances to deliver the daily post. Packages could be delivered more slowly, but with fewer stops.

That Pennytyne and Cyneric kept up with Zapyros at all during the storm was impressive, but now was when things started to really change. Andrés had already dropped out. Anna was going to fall behind. I would be on my own.

So I enjoyed that last night with my friend beside the fire, neither of us saying much, just enjoying each other's company. It was just as novel a feeling for me as that desperate *want* I now carried for Andrés. Everything was changing. Perhaps I was finally starting to find my place in the world. Or perhaps I was just tired. I closed my eyes before I could find out which it was.

The next morning, Zapyros and I flew just as

soon as I'd replenished my supplies from the courier at the checkpoint. Cyneric outpaced us once again, but it wasn't long before Zapyros's steady flying caught him up. I shared one last wave with Anna before the midnight-blue wardancer pulled ahead. Then, we were alone.

We crossed over the northern mountain range of Amontyr in the early morning, Zapyros soaring high over the low peaks and me huddling in my flight leathers against the cold. From there, it was a long journey of hugging the eastern coastline, down to the southernmost tip of the continent and up along the interior of the Torringwich Mountains towards the heart of Greenvale.

Two weeks of flying. We occasionally met another dragon, though none participating in the Great Race, as they went about their courier duties. We saw coastal plains and glass-like lakes, trees whose tops touched the sky and whose trunks were as wide as Zapyros. There were tiny towns where people threw a feast when we arrived, and larger cities where we were greeted with wary caution. There was even a town, Dragon's Hold, that was governed exclusively by dragons. Zapyros liked it there, staying up for most of the night discussing politics with the locals. There were rumours at each checkpoint of where the other transport dragon was, but we never ran into her. Not until Vale's Keep, the capital of the country Greenvale, when Zapyros and I landed midafternoon.

"How are you?" I asked as I slid from the saddle. The last two weeks had been fairly easy for me, though I was weary, but Zapyros looked a little wan, his normally gleaming scales slightly dull. The scratches on his hide had healed without difficulty, but the tiny holes in his wings seemed to be taking longer since the scabs kept falling off during flight. I checked them over before he folded his wings. The spots on the membrane were nice and pink.

"I'm fine," he grumbled, settling down with his tail wrapped neatly around his legs. "The saddle chafes, that's all."

Dutifully, I helped him take it off, making sure the cargo was secure and under guard of his watchful eye before I went into town to ask the local couriers for information. While looking, I wondered how much longer we could do this. Zapyros was a wardancer, and while he was strong enough to finish the race, I wondered at the toll. He was meant to fight, to defend territory or people, not to fly around the whole country without days of rest. He ate well enough, but there was a leanness too him that started to worry me, as well as a listless look in his eyes. I wondered if I should find the local dragon doctor as well, just in case his injuries had been more than mild, then changed my mind at the thought of the scolding I would receive from Zapyros if I did.

The Vale's Keep branch of the Courier's Guild was not hard to find. It was the busiest building on the main thoroughfare, people wearing the Courier blue darting from place to place. I stepped inside and found a harried older woman with grey curls springing every which way at the desk.

"Kayleigh Espinosa," I said, "rider to Zapyros, checking in for the Great Race."

The woman blinked and gaped at me. "You're a dragon rider?"

"Yes?" Usually when I announced that I was rider to Zapyros, people put two and two together. Perhaps she was just having a particularly bad day. "We're camping in the field south of town. If you could have someone bring by a meal and supplies, that would be great."

"Oh, of course!" The woman scribbled something down on a scrap of paper and snapped her fingers at a young man who looked like he had just started his career as a Courier, all wide-eyed and eager. It occurred to me that I'd been that way only a few months ago, and something inside me twisted. How quickly a numbness set in, I thought.

No. No, that was just my weariness from the race. I missed my bed and having a hot bath. I still loved my work. It was everything I had wanted, and more. So why was I staring enviously at the youth as he ran to go deliver my request to whichever inn was supplying for riders during the race?

I thanked the woman and made my way back to the field. Vale's Keep seemed like a pleasant town, full of people and dragons saying hello to one another, a bustling main street, a mild climate for being so near the mountains, trees everywhere. It was almost paradise. Maybe when all this was over, we could come back here and enjoy the sights properly. A rest. Yes, that was what we needed.

Then, I stepped out of the forest-lined path and into the field and my musings vanished, replaced by ice. Jasmine and Victoire were there, the latter standing with her arms crossed, her massive dragon looking haughtily down at the person in front of them. No, not person, *rider*. For there, just paces away from Zapyros, who was standing with wings flared and teeth bared, was a dark green courier dragon that I recognised all too well.

Clover. Which meant that the man talking with Victoire was Markham.

Ice turned into fire and any thoughts of weariness that I had melted away. I ran to Zapyros, letting my legs eat up the ground with ease. He lowered his head closer to the ground and hissed as Clover turned her attention to me.

"What is going on here?" I demanded of Victoire, completely ignoring Markham. She lifted her chin.

"This one is demanding that we give up our place in the Great Race to deliver a package," she scoffed. Jasmine rumbled a low growl, flipping her wings on her back.

Well, it seemed I wouldn't be ignoring Markham any longer. I turned to him and stood there, keeping my expression as smooth as stone. He flinched and hunched his shoulders.

"Courier Espinosa—"

"*Rider*," Zapyros corrected with a snarl.

Markham squeezed his eyes shut. "Rider Espinosa. I need your help."

CHAPTER 25

"I thought you had been transferred to Menaris," I blurted before I had time to think. So much for the placid exterior. It would seem that in the short time since he'd been reassigned, my mask had slipped. I took a breath and smoothed my expression into flat nothingness. Markham watched with a pained look.

"We had a delivery and the local branch of the Guild asked for our help." Clover wove her head back and forth, looking between her rider, Zapyros, and myself.

"*Do not listen to him. The weasel deserves none of our attention,*" Zapyros hissed across our bond. I was inclined to agree with him, but years of conditioning to value politeness were hard to ignore. Not to mention I had a slightly morbid curiosity. What could possibly make him turn to *me* of all people for help?

So I waited, silent. Unmoving. Unexpressive.

Markham shifted his weight. He didn't meet my gaze, which was a change given that I was normally the one with that particular issue. "I know that I have no right to ask, especially not of you. I...I was wrong for the way I treated you. I thought that I was doing you a favour, proving to you how difficult being a courier was going to be with you and Zapyros being..."

"A changeling?" I asked, the words sickly sweet. "A wardancer?"

Markham flinched. Victoire spun on me, eyes wide. "You're Fae Spirited?"

I nodded. She flushed. "Oh. It's just that my brother is Fae Spirited and I thought that, well, never mind. Wait, what does her being a faeling have to do with being a courier?" She narrowed her eyes at Markham.

Faeling? That was a new term to me. I liked it. My estimation of Victoire rose a couple of notches, though I was not entirely sure why she was defending me.

"Nothing. I know that now. And I'm sorry. I

thought that Zapyros wasn't suited for service as a transport dragon—"

Victoire laughed aloud at that. "Not suited? We've been chasing them for weeks! They're always just far enough a head that we miss them. We've had to fly from the moment the sun hits the horizon to when it disappears every night, sleeping away from checkpoints so that we could catch up to you. What about that makes him not suited for this work?"

"It was a foolish bias," Markham said. He exchanged a glance with Clover, who nodded. "We're sorry. Transferring us to Menaris was the right choice."

I folded my hands behind my back. *"Well? What do you think? Are they sincere?"*

Zapyros sniffed Markham once, then drew back, settling down into a crouch, though the tip of his tail still drew deep furrows across the ground, those blades easily gouging the soft dirt. *"They are. And the apology was well said."*

"I accept your apology. We accept."

Markham sagged in relief, nearly swaying where he stood. Clover stepped forward, and he leaned on her for support. "Then you'll help us?" she asked.

"I did not say that." I turned to Victoire, who watched with narrowed eyes. "What do they want?"

"They need a package delivered to some outpost in the mountains. Even though we're exempt from normal delivery while the race is in progress." She scoffed. Jasmine snorted, lifting her chin to look down on Markham and Clover.

"It's medicine," Markham pleaded. "Clover and I can't even carry one full crate, let alone the four that are required. They're having an outbreak of sky sickness and there's no way to get the medicine to them fast enough."

"We could make multiple trips," Clover said carefully. I got the impression that this was not the first time she'd ventured that solution.

"We may have to," Markham breathed. "There's no other way. The pass is too slow to take ponies and we're the only courier pair within miles. Everyone else is worked to the bone with the race taking away so many from regular duty."

"The race is almost over," I pointed out. "Vale's Keep is three days from Ilisar. Can it wait until then?"

Markham shook his head. Clover responded. "We waited two days for you to arrive. Another three to Ilisar, three to return? You two are the only transport class dragons within a week of Vale's Keep; sending for another would take too long. If we can even find one. Imari and her rider retired after Imari lost part of her tail due to an infected flutterling bite."

Jasmine winced. "Imari was the oldest still in service. A noble dragon."

"I hate flutterlings," Zapyros agreed.

"We're not giving up our chance of winning this," Victoire said before I could ask what she thought. "We've waited years to be in the Great Race, and we're this close to winning. Do you know what that would mean? We could have our choice of post. With the prize money, we could—"

"Enough." Jasmine nudged her rider. "We do not need to share with them what we will do when we win."

Zapyros scoffed, sparks floating through the air. Jasmine recoiled as one nearly landed on her snout. "Is that all you care about?" he asked in a low voice. "Winning?"

"Sky sickness isn't fatal," Jasmine retorted. "They'll just be nauseous and not be able to keep their food down for a few days. A week at most. Maybe two."

"And then they'll be weak for months afterwards. Isn't that reason enough to help them?" Zapyros curled his lip in disgust. I wanted to do the same. Sky sickness was enough to leave a person barely able to get out of bed. And while it wasn't fatal in most cases, it often left a person open to other illness while their body recovered. It was a miserable experience and could take many months to recover properly.

"As he said, they can just make multiple trips." Victoire waved a dismissive hand at Markham. "The Great Race only happens once a decade. You have no idea what this means to me, to Jasmine."

"You're right," I said. "I don't. And I don't care. We'll take the medicine."

Zapyros was the one to lift his head now, shooting a superior glance at Jasmine. "As my rider says. No race is more important than seeing such a delivery make it through. Now, where are we flying?"

Clover snaked her head back and forth, exchanging a concerned look with her rider. He nodded. "Caspar Venir," she said. "The medicine is for Caspar Venir."

We set forth from Vale's Keep with the dawn. Zapyros had eaten in large gulps the night before, tearing into his cow with great ferocity. He hadn't even wanted it cooked, just dug his claws in and ate. He also hadn't said anything about it to me beyond directing me to make sure the crates of medicine were doubly secure and wrapped in oilcloth.

I hadn't pushed.

Now, though, as we soared over the Hillsend Basin north of Vale's Keep, I wondered if I should. Jasmine and Victoire were on our tails, though they turned westward while we continued directly north. Zapyros flew with a steady speed that was full of heavy wingbeats, and I couldn't tell whether he was trying to race to deliver the medicine, or if he wanted the whole experience to be over.

"Do you wish to talk—"

"No," he snapped. I flinched back from the bond and reinforced the wall to protect my mind from the sharp emotion that spilled over. Zapyros looked over his shoulder at me. *"Sorry. It's just...I haven't been back to Caspar Venir since they signed the treaty."*

"I thought you said it was just border skirmishes?" I had studied the details of the conflict between Synval and Drimior as soon as Zapyros had told me he'd been stationed at Caspar Venir when we first

bonded. The two countries shared the lake borders, but abutted at Caspar Venir. It had been a contentious piece of territory for generations. I knew it was more than border skirmishes, and he knew it, too.

"*It can hardly be called a proper war if no armies ever fought,*" he said, a hint of bitterness in his tone. "*But they would send dragons, soldiers, raiders sometimes, up to the outpost and we had to defend against them. These last five years were the worst in recent history, which is why they brought a negotiator in from Balastria.*"

He hesitated. I rested my hand on his neck just above the saddle, trying to provide what little comfort I could. "*It was the negotiator who suggested I could be a courier, after...Garret. The others didn't agree with my decision, but the outpost was no longer meant to be a military posting and, well, they didn't need me anymore.*"

"*Still, it was your home for a time, wasn't it?*" I'd only ever seen the outpost on maps, situated between two peaks just shy of the Long Lake and the Drimior border. For the first time, a map felt insufficient. I wanted to know everything.

"*Garret was my home. Caspar Venir was just a place where we lived. And fought.*" Zapyros slowed his wingbeats for a moment as we drew closer to the opposite end of the lake, and the mountains that waited for us. *"Can I tell you something?"* he asked tentatively.

"Anything. You don't need to ask."

He shuddered, his scales rustling hard enough that the saddle shifted slightly. I waited until he was flying straight again to lay my hand back on his neck.

"The only thing you could say that would mar my opinion of you is if you wanted to turn around."

Zapyros snorted fire. *"I would never!"*

"Then you have nothing to fear, right?"

He huffed, another burst of flame lighting the air. I ducked my head to avoid some of the sparks as we flew. "Real mature," I muttered out loud. Zapyros chuckled a rumbling laugh.

"I'm sorry, Little Bird. I could not help myself." A moment later and a trickle of sadness, of shame, came over that shared wall in our minds. *"I never liked battle,"* he admitted. *"I am a wardancer, bred from the finest warriors of dragonkind. Yet I do not enjoy the feel of...of fighting. I never did. Garret, though, now he was a warrior, through and through."* Pride replaced that trickle of shame. *"He knew his calling, and he was unafraid. When he died, though, I felt lost. Being a*

courier with you has been the first time in a long time where I feel like I have a purpose. A chance at being happy."

"*I would never judge you for that!*" I was heartbroken for him, but nothing more. "*You should have a chance to choose what your purpose is in life no matter what breed you are. People can choose their paths, why not dragons? Maybe we can make them see that.*" Winning the Great Race would have done that, I thought with a twinge of regret. It would have made it clear to everyone that Zapyros, a dragon not bred for transport courier work, chose the right path for himself. And we'd given that up for this.

No. I shook my head. Delivering medicine was a worthy cause and I would not feel badly for doing it. And Zapyros didn't need anyone else but himself to validate his chosen path.

"*You know,*" Zapyros said slyly. "*Caspar Venir is a long day's flight from Ilisar. Jasmine and Victoire will be flying slower now that they think we've dropped out. We could still win this race if we hurry.*"

I looked over my shoulder to the dummy crates we'd been assigned for the race. Zapyros had insisted on carrying them, assuring me that the extra weight wouldn't matter and we had to return them to Ilisar anyways. That was his plan all along.

Why he was flying so fast despite being weighed down.

"You sneaky dragon." I grinned. *"Let's do this!"*

Zapyros roared loudly enough to make ripples on the lake below. Then, he started flying faster.

CHAPTER 26

I'd expected the battlements of Caspar Venir, carved into the side of a mountain. I'd expected a fortress, impenetrable and unreachable except by wing. I'd expected a place scarred by fire and scored by dragonclaw.

I had not expected the cold.

"Remind me to pack an extra blanket in the emergency supplies when we get back," I said through chattering teeth as I pulled my singular, too-thin blanket tighter around me. My flying leathers were lined with shearling wool and had kept me warm in all the impossible heights I'd explored, yet here, approaching a fortress in a mountain range that was surely not nearly as high as Zapyros had ever flown, I was freezing.

"I could always light a fire," Zapyros suggested, banking to land. "I'm sure there's something flammable in the crates on my back."

"Ha ha," I deadpanned. Zapyros landed with a graceful click of his talons. Almost instantly, two dragons emerged from a cavern in the cliff, fire at their maws. Suddenly, the cold wasn't the biggest of our problems.

"Intruder!" This was from the female wardancer, her scales a delicate rose shade, though there were many scars of a bright white crisscrossing her hide. She hissed, tail lashing, and I was alarmed to note that she was very nearly the same size as Zapyros. The other dragon was also a wardancer, though he appeared to be just an adolescent and was considerably smaller, with no scars to mar his ice-blue hide.

"I am Courier Kayleigh Espinosa, rider to Zapyros," I called, pulling the Guild flag from its pocket and waving it. At the sight of the Guild colours, the two dragons reared their heads. The female sniffed and bared her teeth, which was decidedly not the reaction I expected to members of the Courier Guild. We were neutral, welcomed by all. Except, apparently, we weren't.

"Impossible," the female wardancer snarled.

Flame danced from her maw. "Zapyros? The traitor to his kind?"

Zapyros growled low in his throat. I spoke up, my voice carrying to echo across the stone fortress. "We have been tasked with delivering medicine to Caspar Venir. I'll need someone to sign for the delivery."

The female lifted her head to me and flicked her eyes to the flag I still held. "Who sends you?" she asked in a clipped tone. "For whom do you spy?"

Spy? I rolled my eyes. "Seriously?" I waved the flag. "No government may use or assume the guise of the Courier Guild for any reason whatsoever; those that would abuse this sacred and *independent* Guild will be restricted from its service, all postal deliveries stopped and restarted only after an official apology and reparations have been made to both the Guild and the wronged courier. Guild Law 17, Section 2. Or do I need to recite the whole code to be taken at my word?"

"She speaks the truth, Titania," Zapyros said in a low rumble. "I have joined the Courier Guild."

"So you turned your back on your kind to play at delivering the post?" Titania scoffed, sparks flying from between her fangs. "You're a worse coward than I thought."

Zapyros hissed, flexing his claws into the stone. The younger wardancer stepped between the two.

"Hey, we need that medicine. Our riders are *sick*, or don't you remember?" He snapped his teeth.

"Fine." Titania spun towards the entrance to the human barracks, her tail lashing, those dangerous blades nearly slicing through a crooked tree growing out of the side of the mountain. "Deliver your package, *courier*. Then you and the blood traitor will leave."

I nearly bit my tongue. "Wow, and I thought Markham was an ass," I murmured. Zapyros snorted, quickly covering the sound with a cough that produced spurts of flame. The younger wardancer looked at us with confusion. I just returned the stare with one of my own, expressionless. He flicked his wings and looked away, uncertain.

Titania rapped a claw on the door to the barracks. A few moments later, the door swung open and a dark-skinned man who looked too ill to be out of bed met her. Titania jerked her head towards us and I waved the Guild flag again. Relief brightened his expression.

"You've come to deliver the sky sickness medicine. I'm Ashar Novis, commander of this outpost," he said, shuffling forwards. I unbuckled myself from the saddle and slid to the ground. His eyes widened in shock for a moment when he saw Zapyros, but he soon schooled his expression. Zapyros seemed to relax slightly.

"I just need a signature and I can get them unpacked for you." I procured the documents and held them still while the man signed a shaky blur of letters. "Do you...do you need help getting everyone their doses?"

He waved me off, though he looked like he could barely stand. "There are a few of us still mobile. We'll get everyone what they need. There's no need for you to stay. I know how uncomfortable this must be for you, Zapyros."

My dragon yawned, showing off his fangs, but he made no answer. Which meant that he was ready to be away as soon as possible. I didn't argue. He lowered himself to the ground, and I unloaded the crates, stacking them neatly by the door to the barracks.

"Good, you're done, now leave." Titania bared her teeth at me, as if that would make me move faster.

Zapyros let out a rippling snarl that echoed across the mountains. "Don't speak to my rider that way." In an instant, he was standing over me, wings spread, scales rattling in a threatening manner. Titania reared back, curling her lip.

"I thought you were a pacifist now," she snapped. "Sworn never to raise a claw again."

"Hardly." Zapyros lowered his head, baring his fangs. If he decided to strike, he would be at her throat in an instant. I held my breath, not wanting to provoke further conflict. I wasn't afraid of Zapyros. I hadn't been since the very first time we met. But there was something savage about Titania that had me feeling more like prey than ever before. "I flew away from fighting some useless war to do something meaningful with my life. That does not mean I will not tear your throat out if you so much as look at my soulbonded wrong."

Titania pulled back, weaving her head back and forth. "You...you soulbonded her?"

Zapyros narrowed his eyes. "I did."

"But she's not a warrior!"

"Do you honestly think that matters to me?" Zapyros growled. A wave of affection flowed over that wall in my mind. I returned it, smiling. "Her heart is pure, her soul true. She is everything that a wardancer could possibly require. What does it matter if she is a courier?"

For the first time since we landed, Titania looked uncertain. She eyed me warily. "It shouldn't be possible. Wardancers bond to fighters because we are fighters," she said at last. The younger dragon stepped forwards, inserting himself between us. Titania blinked in astonishment. "What are you doing, Arctus?"

"Maybe...maybe we can be more than what we were bred to do." He flicked his wings. "Caspar Venir is no longer at war. It hasn't been for a while. We've been doing nothing but flying patrols and hunting to help the mountain villages. I...I've never even *seen* fighting. And when I think of it, I'm afraid."

Titania nuzzled the younger dragon. "Why didn't you say anything?" she asked softly.

"You've been through countless battles. And I'm a wardancer! What wardancer doesn't want to fight?" Arctus stared at Zapyros.

"This one." Zapyros folded his wings and settled into a crouch, relaxing out of his defensive stance. "Yes, our claws and teeth tear better than others. Yes, we can and should fight when the situation demands it. But we can be more. I am a courier. I am flying in the Great Race, and I intend to win."

"But the Great Race is only for transport—" Titania stopped herself. She studied Zapyros, then

Arctus. "Does this...delivering the post, does it make you happy?"

Zapyros nodded and smiled. "It does."

She looked uncertain, shifting her weight. Ashar smiled up at her. "It is okay, my dearest heart," he said, patting her leg weakly. "I know that the call for blood is strong in your veins. But it does not mean that others cannot have a different call."

Titania's gaze softened slightly. She nuzzled Ashar, nudging him back towards the barracks. "Go. Deliver the medicine."

I stepped forwards to help, but Ashar shook his head. "No, courier. I can do this. And you have a race to win, do you not?"

"The sun has started to set," Zapyros rumbled. "If we want to make it in time, we need to leave."

I peered at the horizon. The sun was still high enough that we had maybe an hour's flight before we would have to stop for the night, but we were losing daylight. Fast. And we needed to find a place to camp.

"Thank you," I said to the other dragons, though I didn't quite know why. There seemed to be a weight lifted from Zapyros's shoulders, now that he knew had made peace with his own kind, other dragons he had served with. His past had shaped him, but the future was still his to shape. Ours to shape. He stood tall and proud, neck arced gracefully and tail twitching with eagerness. Before I could even attempt to climb into the saddle, Arctus lifted me into place, his claws gentle around my middle.

"I hope you find your calling," Zapyros said to the younger dragon. "Whatever that may be."

I tapped Zapyros's neck twice once I was strapped in. Without further conversation, he snapped his wings open and leaped off the edge of the fortress. The mountain air caught under his wings and we soared.

"Fly!" Titania called after us. "Fly fast and fierce!"

Zapyros roared in return, his fire lighting the sky. Then, with a twist of his body, and a beating of his wings, we left Caspar Venir behind.

CHAPTER 27

"So." Zapyros picked at his teeth with a talon, trying to dislodge a scrap of fish. We were camped at the edge of Long Lake, just beyond the northernmost peak of the Torringwich Mountains. It had been a bit of a stretch to get there from Caspar Venir, but Zapyros flew fast and true, setting down just as the sun disappeared beyond the horizon.

"So?" I repeated. I stifled a yawn.

"Are we ever going to talk about you and Andrés?"

I choked on a gasp and doubled over coughing. When I could finally catch my breath, Zapyros's nose was inches from mine. "Are you well, Little Bird?"

"Fine," I wheezed. Zapyros sniffed me once then retreated. "Why are you asking about...that?"

"Because you haven't brought it up in the two weeks since we left him and Pennytyne in Varwold. I figured I'd given you plenty of time for you to have thought things over."

"Of course, I would be bonded with a nosy dragon," I muttered. Then, because I didn't know what else to do, I brought my knees to my chest and rested back against Zapyros's side. The warmth of his body behind and the fire before, plus the pressure of the self-hug, calmed my racing thoughts. "It's just...I don't know what it is, to be honest. Between him and me."

"I would have thought it obvious. Andrés wishes to make you his mate."

I nearly started coughing again. Zapyros hummed, the sound vibrating through his scales. "I'm pretty sure that's not what is going on here."

"Don't be ridiculous. Humans have a different word for it, perhaps, but dragons know mating when they see it. What else do you call that thing when your mouths meet?"

I definitely no longer needed Zapyros's warmth, or the heat of the fire; my blushing was enough to keep me warm for days. "Kissing?" I asked, half an octave higher than normal. "It's called kissing. And, I mean, yes, humans usually only do it when they're, ah, dating?"

"Dating." Zapyros snorted. "Ridiculous word. Hardly sufficient. As if setting a date to spend time together adequately describes the relationship between mates."

I shrugged, not quite sure where to look, what to do with my arms. Completely out of my depth. My dragon sighed and wrapped his tail around us as if creating a protective barrier. "I am sorry, Kayleigh. I did not mean to make you feel upset."

"I'm not upset!" I protested. "Just confused."

He tilted his head, eyes gleaming. "Why? It is plain to anyone with eyes that Andrés Mierza has feelings for you. He knows your preferences for touch, for conversation. He accepts and understands your life as a courier, as he is one himself, and I think him more intelligent than most humans. I even like his dragon. Do you not feel the same way?"

I shrugged. "I do. I think. It's just that I've never really, ah, done this sort of thing before. There are not a lot of people who don't mind my, er, oddities."

Zapyros let out a growl that sent ripples across

the waters of the lake and had the fire sputtering. "Then they are fools," he said darkly.

"You're being overprotective." I couldn't bring myself to mind. "Besides, it doesn't really bother me much. I have friends, now. My family, strange as they are. And I have you."

"You will always have me," he assured me. "Maybe, though, you could have Andrés, too? If that's what you want."

Once more, I leaned back against the warmth of his side, all thoughts of embarrassment gone, replaced with a pleasant feeling that had me smiling. "I think, maybe, it is."

"Good. I would hate to have to snub Andrés because he is not good enough for you. He brings interesting snacks in the mornings."

I laughed. "So *that's* why you're always hanging around him!"

"No!" Zapyros pretended to sound affronted. "Not always."

We lapsed into a pleasant silence. I studied the myriad of stars spread across the sky, so beautiful and distant. A navigator's constants, a mapmakers friends. From studying the stars, I could tell exactly where we were. I knew our place on the map I carried in my supplies, and that used to be enough for me to know my place in the world. Now, I thought that maybe knowing my position wasn't the same thing as knowing where I was. Who I was.

"Zapyros?" I said. He turned his great head from where it lay on the grass and opened an eye. "Do you regret choosing me that day?"

"Not for an instant."

I nodded, and that surety of knowing my place settled on me once more. "Good. I don't either."

"Of course not," Zapyros murmured, closing his eye again. "Sleep, Little Bird. Tomorrow will be a long day."

I slept, perhaps better than I had since the race began.

MORNING CAME ALL TOO QUICKLY AND ZAPYROS AND I were in the air just as the sun crested the horizon. We flew as fast as possible, Zapyros's great wings taking scoops out of the air. It was a choppy ride, him being concerned speed more than a smooth ride. Air currents and gusts of wind had him twisting and diving or climbing to high altitude to avoid them entirely. I was grateful I'd eaten nothing more than some bread that morning because I was certain I'd have lost everything in my stomach otherwise.

By mid-day, we'd left the edge of Long Lake and turned northwest, straight towards Ilisar. The landscape blurred beneath us, but occasionally I spotted something that looked familiar.

"*This is right near the path we took to Dun Kennis, isn't it?*" I already knew the answer, the map burned into my head. Yet it felt like an age had happened between my first delivery and this mad dash to win the Great Race.

"*It is*," Zapyros said. "*Keep an eye out for flutterlings!*"

I laughed, throwing my hands into the air. There was no way the flutterlings could catch us, even if they tried. Zapyros chuffed and kept flying. As the trees grew more scarce and the plains opened up before us, he flew lower to avoid the wind at higher altitudes. His shadow raced across the ground and grass whipped from side to side as we passed.

I could tell he was getting tired by the late afternoon. We had made incredible time and by my judgement were maybe half-an-hour from Ilisar. At any moment, we would see the outline of the city on the horizon.

"*Almost there*," I said. Zapyros pulsed a wave of

acknowledgement over the wall, but he was too tired for words. Still, though, his wings beat hard and fast as we raced towards the city. *"Do you think that Jasmine and Victoire—"*

As if my thought had conjured them, I saw a great shadow to the west of us. It was Jasmine, flying much higher than we were, her massive wings letting the wind propel her forward with far less effort than Zapyros was putting out. She seemed to spot us the moment we spotted her; a roar split the sky.

A challenge.

Zapyros didn't bother returning the roar. He just sucked in a great breath, his sides expanding like bellows, and tucked his legs in closer to his body, tail a rudder to his wings. Those, he beat harder. Faster. The muscles in his shoulders and back strained enough that the saddle creaked. I tucked in close to his neck so I could give him any extra aerodynamic advantage, small as it was.

We *flew*.

Ilisar materialised before us as though appearing from a fog. In moments after that, I could make out the details of individual buildings. A road appeared below us, full of people and dragons going to and from the city. As we passed overhead, some of them cheered.

"*You can do it!*" I cried in my thoughts. I pushed as much encouragement through the bond as I could, wishing I could send him my energy as well. Zapyros made no answer, only flew.

Jasmine started her descent, banking so that she was angled towards the field outside the Guild Hall. She was close enough that I could see Victoire on her back, shouting words of encouragement. The transport dragon's wings strained as she tried to beat them faster, but they were meant for endurance, not speed.

Zapyros was meant for both.

Crowds gathered outside of the Guild Hall and along the roads leading to town, probably alerted by a crier or scout meant to watch for our approach. They waved flags in courier blue and screamed cheers as we drew closer. I didn't bother studying their faces too closely, not wanting to hold out hope that my family would be there, that Andrés and Pennytyne would be there.

So suddenly it took my breath away, Zapyros folded both his wings to his side and dropped into a dive. Jasmine was right on our tail. The Guild Hall opened up before us.

Zapyros unfurled his wings at the last possible moment, landing in the middle of the field with an impact loud enough to make me flinch. He tilted his head back, sides heaving from effort, and let out an earth shattering roar.

We won.

CHAPTER 28

"What do you mean we're disqualified?" I asked Master Templeton hoarsely. It was two days since Zapyros and I had returned to Ilisar, and we'd both slept for nearly the whole of yesterday. I had checked on Zapyros this morning after eating a massive breakfast and bathing until my skin was raw. I hated feeling dirty, and the routine of a proper bath was heavenly. Zapyros was still groggy, having gorged himself on food in celebration of winning. I let him sleep.

Now, though, I sat in Templeton's office while being told that Zapyros and I hadn't actually won, that we'd been disqualified from the race entirely.

I clenched my hands into fists to ground myself

while the rest of the world fell away from me. Templeton looked at me with a sad little smile that I couldn't look away from. It was taunting me, laughing at me, and it made tears prick at my eyes.

"Upon arrival, you delivered the dummy crates you were meant to transport through the race, as well as the appropriate paperwork," he said, still giving me that sad smile. He shuffled some papers around on his desk. "You also submitted a delivery form from some supplies you delivered to Caspar Venir? According to the rules of the Great Race, all participants are exempt from deliveries."

My ears roared, and I forced myself to take a deep breath. "We delivered medicine," I said, though it sounded weak even to myself. "And I thought that the exemption was put into place to prevent people from sabotaging the race, waylaying couriers to deliver the post so that their favoured participant could win. It's meant to keep things equal between participants. Isn't it?"

Master Templeton sighed. "Ostensibly, yes. And I am aware that you delivered a much needed supply of medicine in a situation when no one else could. However, the rules remain clear. Participants in the Great Race cannot deliver post for the duration of the race without disqualification."

I normally loved rules. Clean your dishes after eating. Don't steal. When someone says, "Lovely weather we're having," respond with something equally mundane about the weather. Rules as law, rules as boundaries for social interactions. Rules for filling out paperwork. Rules for life. They gave me structure and a guideline for me to follow when the world became too loud, too overwhelming.

Now, though, it seemed like the rules were doing nothing but punishing me.

"There can't be an exception?" I asked, even though I was all but certain of the answer.

"I'm sorry. The winner of the transport dragon class will be Jasmine and her rider, Victoire. You are, of course, still invited to the ball being held in honour of all race participants. And, unofficially, you did arrive first, so you should take pride in that. However..." He trailed off and shrugged helplessly.

"Right. Okay," I said dully. What else was there to do? I could argue, but it wouldn't do much good. I was too shocked to do anything else. So I stood and walked out.

The sunshine outside the Guild Hall felt unnaturally bright. I shielded my eyes and hesitated, not quite sure where to go next. I could go to my room and cry, and a good part of me wanted to do just that. But there was an energy in my limbs that sometimes came from being overwhelmed. So I started jogging. Then I started running.

I didn't have a specific destination in mind, just the need to expend energy. To let my mind process the fact that we'd done everything we could, had even made it to the finish line first, and were still having our success taken away from us. It wasn't fair. Obviously, I knew that life wasn't fair, that there was no guarantee of anything good coming my way, but it still hurt that this one thing I thought I had achieved was ripped from my grasp on a technicality.

Taken away for doing the right thing.

I had no doubt in my mind that if Jasmine and Victoire had been the ones delivering the medicine, their win wouldn't be taken away from them. A raging sadness built in my stomach.

I found myself running up the winding pathways of the hills beside the Guild Hall where most of the courier dragons denned. There were cave entrances at regular intervals and I could tell by the fires in the sconces at each cave whether their occupants were present. I'd never been this way before, never come to see the dragons in their dens. It felt strangely personal, like going to a party I'd not been invited to attend.

Now, though, I followed the bond Zapyros, and I shared to a cave at the top of the hill. It had obviously been recently excavated, as there were signs of the entrance having been widened, not to mention there were bits of rubble strewn about on either side. It was the only cave big enough to hold Zapyros.

I hesitated at the entrance, then shook my head and went in. Surely, after all we'd been through, Zapyros wouldn't mind my showing up unannounced.

The interior of the cave was much nicer than I had anticipated. The floor was actually tiled, the pieces rougher than I usually liked, but which would probably suit Zapyros's claws perfectly. The walls were smooth and had pieces of art hanging on them, each illuminated by a tiny hurricane lantern. There were depictions of famous battle scenes, of dragons, of people. My favourite was a little cottage in a forest clearing where a flock of harrier dragons played in a beam of light.

The hall opened up to a room large enough to be considered a suite for a dragon of Zapyros's size. On one side was a platform with cushions and blankets, the stuffed dog I'd won at the fish festival placed in a position of honour amongst the nest. On the other side was a pit where a fire crackled cheerfully. Before the fire were several handwoven rugs in intricate designs, big enough for Zapyros to sit on. And there, as if conjured out of my need, were Zapyros and Pennytyne, with Andrés lounging on a couch obviously meant for humans. Windcatcher was perched on a natural rock shelf near the fire, her wings spread to warm in the heat.

"Kayleigh!" Andrés shot to his feet. The dragons turned to look at me.

"What is wrong?" Zapyros asked immediately. He extended his neck and sniffed. "Little Bird?"

I shrugged, the words to explain escaping me. Andrés guided me towards the couch, where I sank into the cushions and promptly wished never to move again. Never to emerge from this cavern again. Andrés wrapped his arms around me and held, tightly.

"When did you get back?" I asked. Zapyros frowned, narrowing his eyes at my lack of answer to his question.

"Yesterday. Pennytyne was seen to by a dragon doctor in Dwerheven. We stayed there until she could travel safely, then we took a river barge back here." Andrés smiled at his dragon. She self-consciously licked at a splint on her wing. "Hey! The doctor said to leave it alone."

"I know," Pennytyne sighed. "I will."

Windcatcher leaped from the rock shelf and landed on Pennytyne's back, giving the larger dragon a small nip. Pennytyne snorted. "I'll leave it alone! I promise!"

Andrés chuckled. "They've been doing this since the dragon doctor gave strict instructions for Penny-tyne's care. Windcatcher hasn't let her skip a single dose of medicine, and when she starts doing therapy on the wing, I bet Windcatcher will be leading the effort."

The little harrier dragon preened at the praise. I smiled softly. It was nice to be here, among friends who wouldn't judge me. Who cared about me.

"We heard that you won, though!" Andrés squeezed me a little tighter, grinning broadly. My heart dropped. "Congratulations! My father will be presenting the medals and prize money at the ball. I can't wait to see his face."

"Um," was all I managed before Zapyros broke in.

"They took the prize away from us, didn't they?"

My eyes watered and I bit my lip. Nodded.

"What?" Pennytyne hissed, digging her claws into the rug. Zapyros coughed slightly, and she loosened her grip, but that didn't change the fury in her eyes. Or Andrés's. "How could they do such a thing?"

"We delivered medicine to Caspar Venir. There weren't any other dragons that could take it, not in time to make much of a difference," I explained. "That was against the rules, apparently. Or so they say."

"That's ridiculous!" Andrés looked like he wanted to kick something. Windcatcher flared her wings and hissed, the sound more menacing than I would have expected from the tiny harrier. "Everyone knows that couriers aren't supposed to deliver during the race to prevent cheating, not to withhold medicine. *And* you finished first! How is that supposed to work?"

"We were only tail lengths ahead of Jasmine and her rider," Zapyros sighed. "With our...deviation from the rules, I'm not surprised that they decided to rule in their favour."

"I'm sorry," I breathed.

My dragon snorted. "For what? *You* have done nothing wrong, Little Bird. It is they who took our rightful prize who should be apologising. On their knees, preferably."

"But they won't, will they?" Pennytyne asked. Windcatcher folded her wings, her tail drooping. I was inclined to agree with the sentiment.

"No," Andrés answered when I hesitated. "They won't. Not if I know anything about bureaucracy and politics. They probably won't even make an official announcement, because that will make it seem like they're punishing you. They'll just whisper it into the right ears for gossip to spread across Ilisar and beyond, and then present the prize to Jasmine and Victoire and pretend like you never won."

He was probably right. My stomach dropped even more.

"I was so excited," I managed. The tears I'd been holding off finally arrived, blurring my vision and slipping down my cheeks. I rubbed at them furiously. "And you flew so well!"

"I could outfly them in my sleep," Zapyros said, lifting his chin. "It is no fault of ours that they did this, Kayleigh Espinosa. You know that, right?"

I nodded. I did. I knew it to my core, but it didn't stop what they'd done from hurting.

"I think...I think I won't go to their ball," I said, wiping more tears away. "It would just be rubbing salt in the wound, to stand there and pretend like

I'm okay with it. I've had enough of that to last a lifetime."

"I couldn't agree more," Zapyros said.

"Me, too." Pennytyne beat her tail on the rug. Zapyros threw her a look, but said nothing. Windcatcher launched into the air and flew a circuit before landing on my shoulder and nuzzling up against me. I stroked her soft hide, the pain of rejection dulled by knowing everyone here cared about me. Friends. Family. More.

"I have an idea," Andrés announced. "Why don't we just hold our own ball? We can invite everyone we know. Anyone who we actually want there. And Kayleigh, maybe your dad will lend us the music box? We'll hold it on the same night as the official one, rent out one of the event spaces that isn't being used. Or we just hold it outside. Get someone to do food. Music and food and friends and dancing, no politics, no bureaucracy, no judgement. What do you think of that?"

"I think it sounds wonderful."

A screech from outside caught all of our attention. "The couriers are returning!"

The courier dragons. Anna! I grinned at Andrés, and we both scrambled for the entrance to the cave, Windcatcher flying at our heels, Pennytyne and

Zapyros following more slowly. We emerged into the sunlight just in time to see a red streak followed by a purple and a yellow head for the field outside the Guild Hall.

Cyneric nearly tumbled head over tail in his landing, but despite of the frustrated bark of the yellow courier dragon, there was no doubt in anyone's mind that he had won.

"Come on!" I said, running down the side of the hill. "I'll race you!"

CHAPTER 29

I was nearly out the door with the music box under my arm. The condition of my borrowing it for the night was that it never left my sight, or Zapyros's, and that it had to be transported wrapped in a sheepskin blanket tied around with twine. Even so, Papi had handed it over to me with a smile, saying he hoped I had a good time.

"Kayleigh!" Mami called from the kitchen just as I was about to set foot outside. It was like she had some sort of special sense that told her when I was around and just about to leave. "Come talk with me."

I obliged with less reluctance than I expected. Talking with Mami was better than running around trying to gather up party decorations and food on such short notice. Anna had complained about the lack of proper food for our party all morning. When I pointed out that she could always go to the official ball, she snorted, tossed her hands into the air, and proclaimed, "They can just give me my prize later. Why would I want to go to that stuffy old thing when my friends aren't there?"

"What are you making?" I asked my mother. She was rolling out some sort of dough on the counter, her arms covered in flour up to her elbows.

"Cinnamon dough knots." She gestured to a pile of completed knots off to the side, twisted with perfect art and sprinkled with just the right amount of cinnamon and sugar. My mouth started watering. I loved homemade dough knots. Some of the vendors in the city did a passable imitation, but it wasn't the same.

"Oh, for goodness sakes, Kayleigh, just eat one before you drool on the floor."

I set the music box down—carefully—and took a knot. "These are amazing. Why are you making so many?"

"For your party! Ai, it's such a big argument. Carmen wanted to go to the Guild ball, even when your father explained that you wouldn't be there.

She thinks it will be a good place to rub elbows with high society. Tomas Mierza—the councilman, you know, your friend's father—is giving out the prizes and there will be other high society types present. As if that makes it better after snubbing *my* daughter! Ha!" Mami dug her heels into the dough as if she could personally take out her frustrations on the sweet treat.

My mind, though, latched onto something entirely different. "Wait, Andrés's father is a councilman?"

"Seventh of the Twelve families," she confirmed. The kneading stopped. "Didn't you know?"

I shrugged and shook my head. It would explain why Andrés was worried about being a disappointment to his father. The Twelve were the rulers of Synval, a council voted into power during the rare elections. Once in power, they had a seat for life—unless found guilty of a crime, of course. Tomas Mierza was, therefore, one of the most powerful men in the country. And his son had chosen to become a courier instead of going into a career in politics.

"I'll see you tonight?" I asked, but I was already grabbing the music box and running out the door. Mami called after me, but her call soon died off into a stream of loud grumblings about how no one came to talk anymore. I was outside before I could hear anymore.

"You got the box," Zapyros said approvingly. He was lounging in the front pasture with Grimble by his side, the old herding dragon looking as grumpy as usual.

"I don't see why a valuable piece of this family's history needs to be taken off the property," Grimble muttered. He had one ear twitched towards the cattle in the field behind him, where they grazed contentedly on the rich grass. "We have space here. And then it never needs to leave the farm."

"You really want a hundred people coming here to make noise at all hours of the night, trampling the grass and possibly spooking the cattle if they wander off?" I asked. Grimble huffed.

"No." He lifted his chin. "Why *anyone* would be interested in such an affair, I have no idea."

With that, he strode off, nudging a calf towards its mother. Zapyros snorted. "Friendly sort, isn't he?"

"Be nice. Grimble has been on this farm since before I was born." I climbed into the saddle and secured the music box in one of the saddle bags.

"Did you know that Andrés's family is Seventh of Twelve?"

"Yes." Zapyros stretched his wings out and shook them before leaping into the sky. Grimble let out an outraged noise as the cattle lowed in alarm at the sight of a wardancer so close to them. "I have never met the man, but he sounds disagreeable. Then, power so often goes to humans' heads. Perhaps everything should be run by dragon, as it is in Dragon's Hold."

I fought the urge to roll my eyes. Ever since flying through there on our circuit for the race, Zapyros had taken it into his head that letting dragons be in charge was the only sensible way forward. I quickly learned that arguing politics with him was futile.

"Will he get in trouble for not going to the ball?"

Zapyros considered the question as he winged lazily back towards Ilisar. "I think it likely we're all going to get in trouble for not going to the ball."

I hadn't considered that. I just hadn't wanted to go watch them parade about pretending that what they did was okay. Pretending that Zapyros and I weren't good enough.

"If it were just us not attending, that would be one thing," Zapyros continued. "But you and me,

Andrés and Pennytyne, Anna and Cyneric, plus half the other attendees? They'll be upset. They won't be able to *do* anything, mind, given that any sort of retaliation would be widely known, and then they would have to admit why we weren't in attendance." Zapyros looked smug at this. "They will be angry. And it will be futile, which serves them right."

I couldn't help but agree.

He turned and glided down towards the field across the river from the Guild Hall. We'd convinced the owner to let us hold our party there, provided we help plough it up after we were done. Pennytyne and Cyneric seemed intrigued by the idea of farming, and agreed readily.

Andrés was already setting up, Pennytyne directing people where to put tables for food and the smaller tables for sitting. Windcatcher helped string lengths of fabric along poles set into the ground for decoration. Zapyros landed right in the middle of the field.

"Always have to make an entrance," Andrés laughed as one of the workers carrying a table cursed and dropped the end when Zapyros appeared. "Did you get the box?"

I collected the box and dismounted. "Right here!

I've sworn that it must never leave my sight, or Zapyros's. But we can use it."

"That's great!" Andrés directed me to a wooden platform. "We're going to have some musicians here, and dancing there. Tables around the edges so no one is in the way. And food over there, provided Anna actually returns at some point."

I looked at the space, quickly coming together. By midafternoon, it would be ready for a whole host of people to come and dance, to laugh and to sing, to enjoy themselves. The day was warm, the sky was clear with not a hint of a cloud in sight and the drag-onfire torches set all around the perimeter of the field were keeping most of the insects at bay. It had all the makings of a perfect night.

"Ah, looks like they've started a pile for a bonfire. Of course, it will never burn properly like that," Zapyros said, looking at the collection of wooden scraps thrown off to one side. "I shall teach them the proper method of stacking wood for a bonfire."

He strode off, tail twitching, and cornered several wide-eyed workers who were careful to hide their trembling.

"Are you okay with all of this?" I asked. Andrés threaded his arm through mine and held tightly. My heart warmed. "I mean, your father..."

"He'll be angry," Andrés confessed. "But he was angry when I decided to become a courier instead of something grander. And when I returned home after having to drop out of the race? Well, Windcatcher nearly clawed his face after he yelled at me. I've been staying in Pennytyne's den the last two nights."

"Why didn't you say anything?" I wasn't sure if I wanted to hug him or shake him.

Andrés shrugged. "Because, honestly, I'm used to his disappointment. I know that your family doesn't always understand you, the way you think, the way you see the world. But they love you, regardless, and they support you. My family isn't like that. My father has his plans for the world and my mother is distant. No matter what I do, I'm never going to measure up to their expectations. It took a lot of work to accept that, and sometimes it still hurts, but I have to be okay with the choices I've made in life. They make me happy."

He tucked a strand of hair behind my ear and brushed a feather light kiss on my lips that had me tingling with both want and overstimulation. I kissed him more firmly to get rid of the overstimulation. It didn't reduce the want at all.

"You make me happy," I admitted. "In a way I

never thought possible. I am sorry about your father, though."

Andrés shrugged, then shook his head. "Yeah. Me, too."

This time, I was the one to thread my arm through his. "Well, I'm your family, now. And that means you get the entire Espinosa clan, too. My mother will be thrilled. You're going to have to come to all the holidays, no matter what. Oh, and help with the farm in calving season, probably. Come on, we have a party to plan. We should probably save those workers from Zapyros, too. He takes bonfires very seriously."

Andrés laughed, the sound bright and strong and clear. "Kayleigh Espinosa, you are something else."

I grinned. For the first time, a statement like that made me proud instead of hurt. I embraced that feeling the rest of the afternoon.

CHAPTER 30

"Wow," Anna said when I opened my door on her knock. She had a bunch of red fabric over her arm and was dressed in a gown of green with gold at her throat and waist. Mostly, though, she was staring at me as though I'd done something shocking.

I looked down at my own dress. It was a lilac colour with hints of a darker lavender at the hem and cuffs. Long sleeved and full-skirted, it was both comfortable and swishy, which is why I liked it. I rarely had a chance to dress up, but I was not going to pass up a chance to wear a swishy dress. They felt marvellous. "What is it? Is it my shoes? I don't like heels. I always trip in them and I can't figure out why people would wear them. They're so uncomfortable! I like the slippers better, even though I know that we're having the dance in the field and—"

Anna grabbed my arms, interrupting me. She laughed. "It's not the shoes. They're lovely. You're lovely. Really! You look amazing."

I narrowed my eyes. "Why do you sound so surprised?"

"I'm not!" When I didn't look any less skeptical, she sighed. "I figured you wouldn't have anything to wear, so I brought this dress and I sort of thought that I would help you get ready. You know, hair and stuff. It was going to be a whole thing."

"Oh. You wanted to give me a makeover?" My sister Carmen used to give me makeovers all the time when I was a girl. I hadn't much liked how she did my hair, but I loved getting to wear fancy clothes. Her care had stopped once she entered society and I, very firmly, didn't. "Sorry," I said to Anna. "I can still try on the dress if you like?"

She laughed. "No way! You look great. I just expected, well, okay, if we're being honest, I half expected you to show up in your uniform."

"Why would I wear my uniform to a party?" I frowned, confused. Anna coughed to hide a laugh, her face turning a startling shade of red. Before I could say anything, she had thrown the red dress into my room, grabbed my arm, and pulled me into the hallway, closing the door with a slam.

"Never mind. Doesn't matter. I'll get the dress later. For now, we have a party to get to!"

We made our way to the field outside the Hall, where a sizeable number of people were already wending their way towards the bridge and the glow of the lights in the field beyond. Anna and I turned that direction when a voice called out.

"Oh! Good, there you are." Templeton walked up to us, wearing a fine tunic and doublet of rich sable velvet trimmed in silver. He looked strange out of courier blue, but even more strange was the smile that he wore when he greeted Anna and myself. "I was hoping to find you. Are you ready to go?"

"Go where?" Anna asked before I could.

"Why, the ball of course." Templeton gave a nervous laugh and eyed the people and dragons heading towards the field where we'd set up our own party. "You wouldn't want to be late, now would you? Where are your dragons? They'll be wanted as well."

"Over there," I said, pointing to the outline of Zapyros across the river. He was dutifully watching over the music box and the delivery of food. Cyneric,

I thought, was beside him, sitting on his haunches, front claws scraping the air as he told a story. "Waiting for us."

"Oh, no. No, no, no. You must be going to the proper, *official*, ball to celebrate the Great Race, of course! I heard rumours that there was a competing...event, but—"

Anna interrupted with a wide smile and a flutter of her lashes that had Templeton looking quite confused. "Well, we figured we would throw our own party, since it's obvious that the other one is a farce of political machinations. Why else would they be giving away Kayleigh's rightful prize? Besides, Cyneric and I thought this one would be more fun. Less stuffy. Oh! But you can deliver *my* prize to Cyneric's den. Ta ta!"

She tugged my arm, and we walked off, leaving the administrator of the Courier's Guild gaping after us like a stunned fish. I was speechless, too. My face was on fire and I was certain I tripped over every rock in the field on the way to the bridge.

"That was rude," I said. "Right? I'm not...misunderstanding?"

Anna scoffed, tossing her red hair over her shoulder. "Oh, yeah, that was extremely rude. He deserved it, though. And I wasn't lying, so who cares that I was less than politic? Come on! I see Ferran and I want to brag about my win."

As we crossed the river, it seemed like we also crossed some invisible barrier. The atmosphere became more lighthearted. The people were happier, laughing over food and drinks. The dragons talked with their riders and other attendees. A few even had a crowd of people gathering by them, listening to their stories. The musicians were just starting, tuning their instruments and staring in awe at the music box as it played along with them.

"There you are," Zapyros said, crossing over to me. He tilted his head. "You look nice."

"Why is that such a surprise to everyone?" I threw up my hands and stalked over to the tables of food. My mother was there, depositing her full basket of cinnamon knots. I snagged one before she could smack my hand away.

"Ai! You should eat a proper dinner before you stuff yourself on dessert." Mami looked me over. Her own dress was far more colourful, with full skirts and a ruffled neckline, perfect for dancing. Mine felt plain by comparison. "I like you in purple," she said, nodding firmly. "It suits you."

"Thank you. Where are Carmen and Papi?" I

looked around, but there were already too many people for me to pick anyone out of the crowd.

"Hmmm, I think Marco is with the boys, over there, playing games with the dragons." She pointed to a group of courier dragons, harrier dragons like Windcatcher, and a few other varieties common to Ilisar. They were playing what looked like some sort of ball game with about twenty people. I could tell from a glance that I would never be able to figure out the rules, but they seemed happy pouncing after the ball and each other. Marco had his youngest son on his shoulders; they both whooped with delight as they raced past a dragon.

"Carmen is probably over there," Mami continued, gesturing to a group of well-dressed women who preened and looked at the other guests with a mixture of interest and disdain. "What about your *friend*, Andrés? Where is he?"

I turned in a circle, searching for his familiar face. It was too busy. "I don't—"

"Here."

I whirled, and there he was. Right behind me, looking handsome in a dark tunic trimmed in gold. If you paid attention to that sort of thing, which I decidedly didn't. Mostly. My cheeks flushed as he looked me over and when he took my hand and kissed my knuckles, I thought I might do something so bizarre as giggle.

Thankfully, Zapyros interrupted. He swung his great head over towards the table and took an appreciative sniff. "Those smell wonderful, Madam Espinosa," he rumbled, eyeing the basket of cinnamon knots.

"Would..." Mami hesitated, eyes wide and staring at the various pointed horns and scales Zapyros bore. "Would you like one?"

My dragon looked delighted. "I would, thank you." He opened his mouth, revealing his fangs. Mami looked like she might faint. I smothered a laugh and stepped in, placing a few of the treats on his tongue. Zapyros snapped his jaws shut and considered. "Hmm, is there cardamom in these?"

"Yes," Mami squeaked. "A special ingredient."

"They're perfect. I wonder, do you think they could be made bigger? It is such a bother to try and find a baker who will make pastries for dragons larger than a guarding breed. They say it's too difficult." Zapyros settled in, curling his tail around himself and watching my mother with decided interest. Mami, obviously determining that he wasn't going to eat her, launched into the discussion of dragon-friendly eating with gusto.

"Come on," Andrés whispered, tugging my hand. "Let's make our escape before they notice."

I followed willingly, laughing when he twirled me into the area we'd set aside for dancing. With expert movements, Andrés soon had us weaving between other dancers, dipping and turning and swaying with the music. The music box had no trouble making itself heard over the crowd of people and I happily lost myself in the sensations of the music for a while, matching movement to song.

"Was your father angry?" I asked as we transitioned into a slower dance, Andrés suddenly closer, his hands firm on my waist. "When he learned you weren't going to the official ball?"

"I wouldn't know." Andrés grinned wickedly. "I didn't tell him. And given that I've been staying with Pennytyne the last couple of days, I doubt he found out until tonight, either. I can just imagine the look on his face!"

I snorted inelegantly. "Anna and I ran into Templeton on our way here. I think we're going to get in trouble tomorrow."

"What can they do to you?" Andrés shrugged. He spun me in a circle that had my skirts swishing pleasantly around my legs. "You haven't broken any Guild rules by not attending a ball. At least, I don't think there's anything in the rules about attending official functions."

I blinked. Thought. "No. There's not." And that meant there wasn't a thing they could do to me, not officially anyways. I'd already survived their "unofficial" punishment; I could handle anything else they threw at me.

A weight I hadn't known was sitting on my shoulders lifted and suddenly I felt freer than I had in a long time. Happier, too. I tossed my head back and laughed, the sound carrying over the music box. Andrés joined in, and everything felt perfect. I was a courier, rider to a magnificent dragon, and while getting here had been a battle I never wanted to fight, I wouldn't change anything.

After two, maybe three dances, Andrés let me pull him away. We walked towards the river. The sun had fully set and the lights from the city and from our party twinkled gently on the water.

"Thank you," I said, squeezing his hand.

"For what?"

"This party. It was your idea and we could never have managed it without you pulling everything together. It means a lot to me that you would do this."

Andrés spun me so that my back was pressed

against his chest and his arms were wrapped tightly around me. A hug, warm and secure and just the way I liked it. "Kayleigh, if you must know, I would do anything for you."

"Anything?" I couldn't help but teasing him. Andrés chuckled.

"Okay, well, anything except facing off a flock of flutterlings. Those things are terrifying!"

I laughed. "I won't argue with you there!"

For a moment, we just stood there, watching the gentle waters of the river and listening to the music behind us. I couldn't bring myself to care that they were taking away my prize for winning the Great Race. That they had done everything they could to try and make me fail, make Zapyros fail. We had succeeded against all odds. And more than that, we'd found a place in the world.

"Do you ever wish you could have picked another path?" I asked. "Something other than being a courier?"

"No," Andrés answered immediately. "I think I'm exactly where I'm meant to be."

"Yeah." I smiled, broad and wide and honest. "Me, too."

CHAPTER 31

Two days later and it was almost like the Great Race had never happened. The allotted rest period for all participants had passed and so Zapyros and I were in the field outside the Guild Hall, having our gear checked over by the leatherworkers before we accepted another assignment.

"What happened?" the man working on Zapyros's saddle, Casey, asked in dismay. He was short, stocky, and held his tools like they were extensions of his body. He also hadn't flinched at the sight of Zapyros. I liked him. "It looks like you were attacked!"

Zapyros snorted, rolling his eyes. "Hardly. I

caught a courier dragon as she fell from the sky. If I'd been attacked, this would have sustained considerably more damage."

Casey made a strangled noise in the back of his throat. He climbed all over the saddle, muttering to himself and glaring at Zapyros, who watched from a safe distance, so as not to further incur Casey's wrath. He tested the saddle bags and the stitching on the straps for the seat. Finally, he huffed and clambered to the ground. "The saddle is sound for flying and for transport. But I recommend getting those scratches fixed. They're so unsightly!"

I pressed my mouth together to keep from laughing at the indignation on Zapyros's face. He huffed, affronted. Then, more tentatively, he said, "Actually, I want to order a new saddle. This one is standard for the Aerial Corps and I want something lighter, more manoeuvrable."

"A new saddle? I thought you liked this one. It's comfortable, isn't it?" My eyes strayed to the seat where Garrett had carved his name so long ago. Zapyros followed my gaze and sighed.

"It is a remnant of a life I no longer lead. I saw the saddle that Jasmine wore and it seemed better suited for being a courier." Zapyros lifted a talon and ran it over the engraving on the seat. "Even if the memories this one holds are strong."

Casey followed where we looked. "I can always incorporate pieces of the old one into the new. Of course, it will take about a month to make something for a dragon of your size. I'll need to take measurements and see how you fly. How your rider sits."

"Naturally." Zapyros waved his tail dismissively. "It must suit Kayleigh perfectly. Both sitting upright and laying flat, for longer journeys. And it needs a place to store her supplies within easy reach of the seat."

Casey pulled out a notebook from one of his seemingly endless pouches on his tool belt and started scribbling down information. He asked Zapyros to spread his wings, to stand and to sit, then walked all over the old saddle again. I let my eyes glaze over when they started discussing aerodynamics, instead looking out over the field.

Other dragons were arriving for the start of their shift, some still yawning, others chewing the last of their breakfasts. Their riders appeared with bags of mail over their arms, greeting their companions warmly.

Anna and Cyneric landed, looking bright and eager, as if they'd already been out for a morning flight. The red dragon was looking much recovered from the long-distance flying of the Great Race, and Anna looked much better compared to yesterday's hangover. I waved.

"Did your prize get delivered?" I asked. "What was it?"

The two gaped at me.

"What?"

Anna clapped a hand over her mouth, stifling a giggle. Cyneric, though, was bold enough to ask, "Are you telling me that you flew the entirety of the Great Race without even knowing what the prize was?"

I shrugged. "Zapyros wanted to win, so that was reason enough for me to fly. Why? Is it important?"

"It's only enough coin to equal about three years' worth of salary!" Anna blurted. "Not to mention every craftsman in the city falling over themselves to work on our gear, just to say they work with the winner of the race. I won't have to pay for repairs for ages!"

"Oh. I guess that's good." Certainly having that much coin would have been useful, though I didn't really know what I would do with it. I didn't need new lodgings or clothes or anything. Maybe I would have bought some new mapmaking supplies.

Cyneric twisted his head around to exchange a look with Anna. Then, gently, he nuzzled me in the chest. "You are a strange person, Kayleigh Espinosa. I like you."

I patted the smooth scales of his muzzle. "Thank you? I like you, too."

Zapyros made a gentle growling sound from somewhere above me. Cyneric jumped and pulled back, his wings tight against his side as he backed down from the massive wardancer. I looked up at my dragon. "Did you know about the prize?"

He shrugged his shoulders, his wings fluttering at the movement. "It's just coin. I have plenty of that after my time in the Corps. I just wanted to win. And I did!"

I patted his leg. "Yes, you did. No matter what they say."

Someone coughed behind me. I whirled. It was Master Templeton, wearing his official robes and looking uncomfortable. He refused to meet my gaze, which was odd, as that was usually my problem. "Good morning, Rider Espinosa."

Zapyros growled, deeper this time.

Templeton paled. "Zapyros. Always a, ah, pleasure."

"How can I help you?" I asked, not bothering to hide my confusion. "We haven't had our morning deliveries sorted out yet, if that's what you're coming to talk with us about. There's been a delay."

He bobbed his head in a nod. "Oh, yes, no, that's perfectly fine. I, um, actually came to talk to you about..."

"Yes?" Zapyros asked imperiously.

Templeton flushed a bright red. He tugged on his uniform as if he needed the reminder that he held a position of power. "After some discussion, it has been decided that the Courier Guild will now be opening applications for all dragon-filled positions to any breed that, ah, wishes to join."

I frowned. "Wait, that means—"

"Transport dragons and courier-bred dragons will no longer be the only breeds allowed to join the Guild." Templeton nodded firmly, as if that answered any questions, and shuffled back. He froze when Zapyros lowered his head, fixing him with a great amber eye.

"Why the sudden change?" my dragon asked. "You only accepted my transfer from the Aerial

Corps because of a shortage of transport dragons, most being too old or busy with breeding."

If it was possible for Master Templeton to look even more uncomfortable, then he did. He mumbled something too quiet and quick for me to make out. Zapyros understood, though, and he tossed his head back and laughed, spurts of fire filling the air. Templeton gave a shallow bow to us and scurried off.

"*What?*" I asked him. "*What did he say?*"

"The other transport dragon, Jasmine?" Zapyros chuckled, still spitting sparks. "She and her rider took their prize money and retired! They bought some land near Fenwood and have quit the Guild. I'm the only transport-class dragon left! If they don't bring in other breeds, there will be an end to that part of the Courier Guild, and they will lose all the revenue that comes with it."

Cyneric snorted. "No wonder they opened applications."

"Well, Kayleigh, they may not have given you your prize, but surely the poetic justice counts for something," Anna said. I found myself smiling along with her.

"I think it rather does."

Just then, a group of people bearing a laden

wagon came into view, led by a woman in Courier blue, barking orders. Zapyros sighed and shrugged his worn saddle over his shoulders. I dutifully went about buckling it in anticipation of the morning mail.

Andrés and Pennytyne walked down from the dragons' hill as the workers were loading Zapyros's saddle bags and I was dealing with paperwork. "Hey, looks like the morning post has finally arrived."

"We've got another delivery for Dun Kennis," I said, gesturing to the crates. "Plus a few pieces for Virias. Looks like we'll be away for a few days."

Andrés ignored the waving of my pen and stepped in close, kissing me before I knew what was happening. I forgot all about the paperwork.

"Ahem." The courier handling the loading of Zapyros's saddle folded her arms. I handed over the paperwork. "Thanks." She stalked off.

"Pleasant sort," Andrés commented, watching her go. He turned back to me. "Did you hear the news?"

"We did." Zapyros looked smug, curling his claws into the soil. If he'd been a cat, he'd be purring. "Administrator Templeton told us the news himself. I really appreciated the personal delivery."

"Oh, hush," I scolded. "You just liked watching him squirm."

"It was very pleasant."

Andrés shook his head. I tried to hide my smile, but failed. Miserably. "Pennytyne and I are going to be reviewing the applications until we're cleared to fly again."

"And I will battle any who fail my questions!" Pennytyne announced. Windcatcher landed on her head and bared her teeth ferociously. Andrés sighed.

"As you see, I still have to figure out the entrance criteria. There have never been any for dragons, just humans, so this should be...fun."

We all watched Pennytyne and Windcatcher run around after each other, the smaller harrier dragon flitting between Pennytyne's legs and swooping high overhead. Zapyros huffed and blew a narrow stream of fire between the two wrestling dragons. They halted, wide-eyed.

"Perhaps you could act with the dignity of our kind?" he asked, humming. "After all, you have been tasked with a challenge of great importance. Delivering the post is a sacred duty, bound by neutrality and with loyalty only to the Guild. Not all are suited for such a life."

Pennytyne tossed her head. "As if we would forget that!"

Windcatcher landed on Andrés and rubbed her head against his cheek. He gave in and scratched her chin. "We'll be sure to screen all applicants thoroughly," he promised Zapyros.

"Good. Now, Little Bird, hadn't we better be going?" Zapyros crouched down for me to climb into the saddle. Andrés snagged my hand before I could, and pulled me in for one more kiss. I really couldn't complain. "Anytime, now!" Zapyros called.

I broke away and climbed into the saddle, strapping myself in. "All set."

"Good." With a sweep of his wings, Zapyros took to the skies. The Guild Hall quickly fell away, becoming nothing more than a speck at the edge of Ilisar, the city itself a note on a map. I leaned into the saddle and let the wind dance over my face before I snapped my goggles into place and put the muffs over my ears.

Once upon a time, all I wanted was to trace the lines of my maps with my feet, running the streets and delivering messages until I knew every scrap of ground, every bit of dirt, every corner and building just as well as I knew the maps. Now, though, the world lay before me in bright jewel tones. The sun warmed my face and the steady beating of Zapyros's wings soothed me. I could feel his happiness through our bond, and sent back my own.

Yes, this was much better than running around the city. Instead of being surrounded by bustle and noise, I faced a wingswept sky with Zapyros at my side. I wouldn't exchange it for anything.

ABOUT THE AUTHOR

Evelyn Grimald Stone is an independent author, editor, and linguist who has been writing, creating and causing vast amounts of trouble since a young age. She has published more than twenty novels in the fantasy genre and has several more in the works. When not writing, she is off musing about the workings of languages—both real and created—or reading, drawing, or sewing. She lives with her two cats and two dogs, all of whom provide endless inspiration for her stories.

Also by Evelyn Grimald Stone

Song of Ink Duology

In Memoriam Duology

The Wing Cycle Trilogy

On Behalf of Death Series

The Crow and the King

The Order of the Owl

Speaker of Words